THE COASTWATCHER

THE COASTWATCHER

Elise Weston

PEACHTREE
ATLANTA

Ω

Published by
PEACHTREE PUBLISHERS
1700 Chattahoochee Avenue
Atlanta, Georgia 30318-2112

www.peachtree-online.com

Cover design by Loraine M. Joyner
Book design by Melanie McMahon Ives

Photo credits: p. 126, German U-boat, courtesy of the National Archives; p. 128, German POWs, courtesy of U.S. Coast Guard; p. 129, Defense at Sea poster, by permission of the Library of Virginia; pp. 130–131, family photos courtesy of the author

Printed in August 2010 by Lake Book Manufacturing in Melrose Park, Illinois, in the United States of America

10 9 8 7 6 5 4 3 2 (hardcover)
10 9 8 7 6 5 4 3 2 (trade paperback)

Library of Congress Cataloging-in-Publication Data

Weston, Elise.
  The coastwatcher / by Elise Weston.-- 1st ed.
    p. cm.
  Summary: While eleven-year-old Hugh, his family, and his cousin Tom are spending the summer of 1943 on the South Carolina shore to escape the polio epidemic, Hugh uncovers clues that point to a German plot to sabotage a nearby naval base.
  ISBN 13: 978-1-56145-350-4 / ISBN 10: 1-56145-350-1 (hardcover)
  ISBN 13: 978-1-56145-484-6 / ISBN 10: 1-56145-484-2 (trade paperback)
  1. World War, 1939-1945--South Carolina--Juvenile fiction. [1. World War, 1939-1945--United States--Fiction. 2. Family life--South Carolina--Fiction. 3. South Carolina--History--1865---Fiction.] I. Title.
  PZ7+
  [Fic]--dc22
                                           2005010816

For Bill,
and for my brother Jay
—E. W.

Special thanks to Fritz Hamer, Curator of History,
the South Carolina State Museum; Hugh M. James Jr.;
Major General Perry M. Smith; Cathy Fishman,
Laurie Myers, Sherri Rivers, and Nancy Benjamin;
and to my editor, the patient and gentle Vicky Holifield.

Chapter One

August 1943

At first it was just a speck out in the ocean. A porpoise's fin, or maybe a piece of driftwood. No, it was moving along too fast, too straight, on a course parallel with the beach. He could just make out the tiny wake splashing along behind it.

He took the binoculars away and rubbed his eyes. When he looked back, it—the thing—was still out there, and coming closer all the time. Suddenly he was all goose bumps, even out here in the broiling hot sun.

The sea oats behind him rustled, and he jumped. Jiggs, his cocker spaniel, nosed something in the sand, scratched himself, and flopped down. "Jiggs," he whispered as the thing out in the ocean passed right in front of them. "It's a periscope! I know it is!"

"Hugh!" his mother called from the front porch. "Hugh! Time to come in!"

Not yet, Mama.

Sweat trickled down his face. His eyes were burning, but he kept them glued to the black speck out in the ocean. Now it was hardly moving at all.

Jiggs got up and shook himself, peppering the boy with sand. "Thanks," Hugh muttered. He closed his eyes to rest them for just a second, and when he looked back through the binoculars, the periscope—that's what it was, it *had* to be—was gone. His heart thumped. He adjusted the binoculars and swept the horizon, all the way down to the south end of the island and back. Nothing. Not even a seagull. Just empty sea and empty sky.

"Hugh! Right this minute!"

He sat up. "All right!" he yelled. "I'm coming!"

As he came down the boardwalk from the beach, Mama called from the top of the porch steps, "Aren't you overdoing it? You've been out there with those binoculars for almost two hours."

He shrugged and started up the steps.

"Oh, no, you don't," she said. "Go wash off that sand."

"Mama—"

"Go."

He sighed, handed her the binoculars, and headed for the shower under the house. The house was built up high off the ground so the breezes could "circulate." Not much was circulating on this hot day, so the cold water felt extra good, especially around his eyes where the binoculars had rubbed the skin raw.

When he came shivering up onto the porch, Mama was waiting with a towel. "What did you see today, Mr. Coastwatcher? A German submarine?"

He caught his breath. But when he looked up at her, she was smiling, shaking her head a little bit. Teasing him.

She wrapped the towel around him and gave him a hug. "Hurry up," she said, and went inside.

Hugh looked back out at the ocean. Nothing there. Wait—there was the osprey, the one that lived back in the marsh, hovering low over the water, hunting for its supper.

"Hugh!"

He scanned the ocean one last time. *Something* was out there, even if he couldn't see it right now. And whatever it was would be a secret. His secret.

* * *

From his place at the supper table Hugh could see Abram fishing out in the creek. Behind the old man the sun was setting, turning the marsh gold and silhouetting Abram so he seemed blacker than he already was. He was standing in the middle of his boat, poling it along. Looking for flounder.

"There's Abram," Hugh said, but nobody heard him. They were talking about polio again. Hugh wished they'd shut up.

"A boy in our neighborhood got it," Tom was saying. "We all had to be quarantined." Tom was Hugh and Sally's first cousin from Atlanta.

"Gosh, how did you stand it?" Sally said. Her tone of voice made being quarantined sound wonderful.

Ever since Tom arrived two days ago, Sally had been acting stupid. Tom was thirteen, a year older than Sally and a little more than two years older than Hugh, but he tried to act like he was about twenty. He thought he was *so* great just because his father was in the Navy and getting ready to ship out from Norfolk, Virginia. Tom was staying with them until his mother—Mama's sister Ellen—got back from seeing his father off. His cousin was supposed to be at camp in North Carolina, but it had been canceled because of the polio epidemic. Tom's older brother Joe was staying with a friend in Atlanta.

Hugh hated hearing about polio. He and Sally and their mother had been here at the beach all summer to get away from it. There'd already been about a dozen cases in Charleston. Not long ago he'd read a story in *TIME* magazine about some doctors who thought flies might be the carriers of polio. They'd mashed up a bunch of flies and fed them to monkeys to see if the monkeys got polio. It sounded horrible—how would those doctors like it if they had to eat flies? And then got polio?

"Mostly the quarantine was boring," Tom was saying. "We couldn't go swimming or to the movies or anything."

"Did the boy die?" Sally said.

"No, but he can't walk," Tom said.

Hugh felt like putting his hands over his ears. He looked back out at the marsh. "Abram got a flounder," he said. But nobody else even looked.

Chapter Two

Hugh lay in the dark, listening for the sound of his father's car. Earlier, Daddy had called from his law office in Charleston to say he was on his way. He hadn't been to the beach in almost a month. Gas was rationed, and it took a whole tank to drive the seventy miles from Charleston and back. Daddy always got there late because you weren't allowed to go over thirty-five miles per hour. Lots of things were different because of the war.

Even though Hugh had only been nine years old at the time, he remembered clear as anything the day the war began for the United States—Sunday, December 7, 1941. It was in the afternoon. They were all in the living room, at home in Charleston. Daddy and Mama were listening to a concert of classical music on the radio, and he and Sally were lying on the floor, playing Parcheesi. Jiggs was a little puppy then. He'd just sat down in the middle of the Parcheesi board, scattering the pieces everywhere. Hugh and Sally were laughing when suddenly the music on the radio stopped.

"We interrupt this program for a bulletin," an announcer said really fast. "Japanese warplanes are bombing the U.S. fleet at Pearl Harbor in Hawaii." Hugh caught his breath. His father was leaning forward in his chair, his fists clenched.

"We'll be in it now!" Daddy shouted.

The next day, President Roosevelt went before Congress and asked that war be declared on the Japanese Empire. He said that Sunday, December 7, 1941, was a date that would "live in infamy." Four days later, Germany and Italy, Japan's allies, declared war on the United States.

In his speech, the President had said that the United States was in "grave danger," and in the days after Pearl Harbor that danger seemed very real, even in Charleston. People jumped at loud noises—the wail of an ambulance siren, a car backfiring. On the radio, Mrs. Roosevelt told parents how to make a "game" of possible bombing raids. When a child heard a loud explosion he was to say "Boooom!" This was supposed to keep the child from being frightened if there was a real bombing.

"Oh, *really*," Mama said when she heard about Mrs. Roosevelt's game. Daddy laughed, but Hugh thought it might be a pretty good idea. He tried yelling "Boom!" at the top of his lungs one night during a thunderstorm. It worked—sort of. Except that Sally came flying into his room, hollering, "Are you crazy, Hugh?"

After the United States entered the war, it seemed as if just about every man in the country was joining up. The recruiting stations were open seven days a week, day and night. Daddy tried to enlist in the Navy and then the Army and then the Marines. But none of them would take him because he was deaf in one ear from getting hit by a base-ball when he was a teenager.

As a last resort Daddy tried the Coast Guard. When he came back to the house that afternoon, he slung his hat across the room. It skidded across a table and almost knocked over a lamp. Jiggs yelped.

"Jack!" Mama gave him a dirty look.

"Sorry." He sank down into his favorite armchair. "The Coast Guard didn't want me, either." He sat there for a few minutes, and then suddenly he started laughing. "I talked with an old man there," he said, "an eighty-one year old who'd been a major in the Spanish-American War. Charged up San Juan Hill with Teddy Roosevelt. He was trying to enlist today, too. If they'd taken *him*, I don't think I could have stood it." He laughed again, but Hugh knew how disappointed he was. Most of his father's friends were already in uniform.

Daddy ended up in Civil Defense. All he had for a uniform was an armband with a triangle on it with the letters CD inside. His main job was to go around after dark and check to see that people's blackout curtains were pulled. The government had ordered people to put up blackout curtains so that if enemy airplanes flew over, the pilots couldn't see any lights down below. Those curtains were a pain sometimes. They were extra heavy to block out the light, which was okay in the winter. But in the summer, when they also blocked any breezes, they made it stifling.

Now the lamp on Hugh's bedside table was turned off and the curtains were open, but there wasn't much breeze. Overhead the big ceiling fan was thumping away. Hugh could barely hear the waves breaking out on the beach. He closed his eyes, and again he saw that little black speck out in the ocean with the white wake splashing along behind. The periscope. Maybe he'd tell Daddy about it. *He* wouldn't laugh.

Then he must have gone to sleep, because he didn't hear the car. The next thing he knew, his father was leaning down to give him a good-night kiss. "Daddy," Hugh said, only half awake. "I saw something today. Out in the ocean."

Daddy turned his good ear toward Hugh. "What's that, son?"

"I saw something through my binoculars." He hesitated a moment, then blurted it out. "It was a periscope, Daddy, I'm sure it was. And it was in pretty close."

"A periscope, huh? Are you sure it wasn't a—"

"Daddy, it was a periscope."

"Well, tell me if you see it again," Daddy said, stifling a yawn. "I've got to go to bed. I'm beat."

As his father walked into their bedroom across the hall, Hugh heard Mama say, "Is he still awake?"

"I'm afraid I woke him up," Daddy said. "He told me he'd seen a periscope today. Does that mean he's still coast-watching?"

"Every day. Sally gave it up long ago. Said it was too hot and too boring."

"Who knows, Hugh might just see something."

"I certainly hope not," Mama said.

Hugh sighed and put his hands behind his head. He lay listening to the katydids and the sound of the waves and the ceiling fan going *thunk-a-thunk-a-thunk.*

Chapter Three

The next morning Hugh went crabbing with Abram. All around the boat the green marsh spread out, the creek winding and winding through the long grass like a shiny blue ribbon. Mullet jumped, long-legged herons fished in the shallows, and crabs scuttled around near the banks of the creek, just waiting to be caught.

And right then a crab tugged at Hugh's line. "Get it, Hugh!" Abram whispered.

Inch by inch Hugh pulled up the line. "It's a big one, Abram," he said softly. "Look at the way it's pulling."

"Just pull him steady, Hugh, you'll get him. Yessir, yessir, Hughboy, you going to get him." Abram had caught thousands of crabs, but each new one seemed more exciting to him than the last.

Pulling this one in was taking forever, but then there it was, just below the surface, the green-brown back, the big blue claws. In a lightning-fast swoop Abram reached down with the net and scooped up the crab.

"That's the king of the day, Hugh," Abram said. "Oh, fine!" He reached into the net and grabbed the crab by its back flippers. "What you got in your big old claw, Mr. Crab?" He pried a tattered package out of the crab's red-tipped claw and sat staring at it, shaking his head. "Look here. Looks like old Mr. Crab smokes cigarettes." He handed the package to Hugh. "What's this? Ain't no Lucky Strikes."

Hugh stared at the limp package in his outstretched hand. It couldn't have been in the water very long, because the two cigarettes in it were still whole. He'd never seen the brand before, red and black writing on a white background. There was something familiar about the heavy, crooked black letters...something he'd seen at the movies on *March of Time*, the newsreel that came on before the feature. He caught his breath, and for the first time that day he thought about the periscope. He eased the damp package into his shirt pocket. "Abram," he said, "I think it's time for me to go in."

* * *

Mama made them all rest for an hour every day after lunch, even Tom. It was because of the polio—she didn't want them to get "overtired." When Hugh got up to his room after lunch, he took the cigarette package off the windowsill where it had been drying and wrapped it up in some Kleenex. Then he slipped it into his scrapbook between two pages of photographs from *LIFE* magazine of captured U-boats—German submarines.

He'd been working on the scrapbook for a year and a half now. On the front he'd drawn a big American flag. Inside were photographs and articles he'd cut out of magazines and newspapers. The first section was called "The Allies." It had pictures of the Allied leaders: President Roosevelt of the United States, Winston Churchill of Great Britain, and Joseph Stalin of Russia. After that Hugh had included photos of Allied military commanders like General MacArthur and Admiral Nimitz and Great Britain's General Montgomery. The next section had pictures of The Enemy—Hitler and Tojo and Mussolini. In the back he had pasted articles about airplanes and tanks and ships and artillery. Sometimes he got in trouble because he cut things out before Mama and Daddy had a chance to read them. He had shoe boxes full of clippings.

He closed the scrapbook and stood staring out the window, itching to get back out on the beach.

"Time's up!" Mama called. "Siesta's over."

Hugh flew down the stairs, grabbed the binoculars off the hat rack by the front door, and dashed outside. He threw himself down on a sand dune and scanned the shoreline. Two shrimp boats on their way in, a flock of noisy gulls trailing in their wake, a lone black Labrador retriever moseying down the beach. That was it. He made two more sweeps of the ocean with his binoculars. Nothing. He wiped the sweat from around his eyes and rested his chin on his folded arms. By now he'd learned to be patient.

It had been a lot different last summer. In the first seven months of 1942, German U-boats had sunk several hundred Allied ships just off the Atlantic coast, from up in Newfoundland all the way down to Florida. President Roosevelt called the U-boats "the rattlesnakes of the Atlantic." There had been a terrifying incident down in Georgia when two oil tankers were torpedoed off St. Simons

Island. The force of the explosions had shattered window-panes as far as eighteen miles inland. Local people had gone out in boats to help rescue some of the sailors, but nineteen of them had died. On some beaches, the Coast Guard had organized horse patrols to help keep a lookout.

That June, as soon as they got to the beach when school was out, Sally and Hugh had started coastwatching. They'd kept watch every day, taking turns with the binoculars, but they'd never seen anything suspicious. Now, a year later, Sally had lost interest. Not Hugh. Things were much quieter along the Atlantic coast, but who knew? Something might happen.

Something was happening now. That thing he'd seen yesterday was a periscope. It had to be! He wriggled farther down into the sand. Next to him, Jiggs sighed. In a little while the dog got up, shook himself, and trotted off.

Two hours later, Hugh gave up, too, and headed back toward the house. Tom and Sally were sitting on the front steps, Jiggs lying at their feet. When Hugh came trudging up the steps, Sally looked over at Tom and laughed. "Here comes the coastwatcher," she said. Tom glanced up, then went back to reading *LIFE* magazine.

It was pretty amazing how much Sally and Tom looked alike—both blond, blue-eyed, and muscular. They looked more like brother and sister than Sally and Hugh did. Hugh was more like Daddy, with dark hair and eyes. And skinny.

Sally was strong as a mule. She could outrun most of the boys in her class. When Sally and Hugh were younger, one of her favorite tricks had been to sit on him and twist his arm behind his back. But he had a secret weapon—he was smart. He'd figured out pretty quick how to stay one step ahead of Sally. And they'd gotten along fine all summer—until Tom came.

Hugh sat down on the step next to Sally and brushed the sand off his legs.

"What are coastwatchers, anyway?" Tom said.

"Oh, that's just something Hugh made up," Sally said.

"I did not!" Hugh shouted. "That's a big lie, and you know it!" He looked over at Tom. "You really don't know?"

Tom shrugged. "No. I can guess—somebody who watches what's happening on the coast. Is there more to it than that?"

"We got the idea from hearing about the coastwatchers out in the Pacific, on those islands," Hugh said. "People like missionaries and coconut planters and traders. They provide intelligence about the enemy—what Japanese ships might be doing, that sort of thing."

"Yeah," Sally said. "They have special short-wave radios and secret codes and all. Hugh eats up that kind of stuff."

"Hey, Hugh," Tom said. "How about teaching me your secret code?" He was grinning.

Sally laughed. Hugh could have smacked her. Last summer she had been just as excited about coastwatching as he was. He got up and went inside, slamming the door behind him. He avoided Tom and Sally for the rest of the afternoon. Right after supper he excused himself and went to his room.

* * *

Something woke Hugh up. A mosquito, or Jiggs down at the end of the bed, scratching a flea. He knew it had to be after midnight because the house was so quiet. Maybe he was just thirsty.

He went into the bathroom, pulled the blackout curtains shut, and turned on the light. He was starting to fill a glass with water when he noticed Tom's shaving kit lying on top of the wicker clothes hamper. It was the first time he'd seen it. It looked almost exactly like Daddy's, leather with a zipper, except Tom's was brand-new, and it had initials on it in gold—TMF, III.

Hugh carefully unzipped the kit. There wasn't much in it—a toothbrush, toothpaste, a hairbrush. He pulled the kit open wider and saw a razor. There was no blade in it, and the little package of blades in the kit was unopened. He picked up the razor and pretended to give his cheek a couple of swipes. Then he put it back. The only other thing in the kit was a jar of Mum deodorant. He gave his underarm a little sniff. A little salty, maybe, but not bad. Still, he put a tiny dab of Mum under each arm, just for kicks. Then he zipped the kit back up and finished filling the water glass. He turned off the light, went back to his room, and stood at the window, sipping his water and looking out to sea.

The moon was out. It was nearly full. The tide was high, the waves crashing against the beach. Things were white on black, like in a photograph negative. There was just a little breeze—the sea oats were barely moving.

The moon went behind a cloud just for a moment, but then the cloud moved and Hugh saw a little flash of light out in the water.

Chapter Four

Hugh held his breath. Something was out there. Something moving sideways. And it was in close. Even without binoculars Hugh could see the rippling white wake on the moonlit sea. He felt the hair rise on the back of his neck.

He went to his door and stood there for a moment listening, his heart beating fast. All he heard was the thumping of the fan overhead and Jiggs scratching himself. He took a deep breath and then he slipped downstairs, Jiggs jingling along behind him. He grabbed the binoculars and went out on the porch. Standing at the top of the steps, he gazed out toward the water.

The thing was still out there, moving very slowly now. He could see something black sticking up out of the water just ahead of the wake. He stepped back into the shadows.

Suddenly Hugh was shivering. He hurried back inside. From halfway up the stairs he heard Jiggs barking outside. "Shoot!" he muttered.

He went back down and let Jiggs in. Then he ran softly upstairs to his parents' room and eased their door open.

Daddy was lying on his back, his arm over his eyes, snoring a little.

"Daddy!" Hugh whispered.

His father groaned and started to roll over. Hugh shook his arm. "Daddy! Please wake up!"

Daddy sighed. "What is it, son? A nightmare?" He patted Hugh's back. "Go on back to bed. You'll be fine—"

"Daddy! It's the sub! The one I told you about!" He was trying to whisper, but it wasn't working. "It's out there— you have to see—please get up! Hurry!"

"Oh, Hugh…" It was Mama.

"Now you've waked your mother," Daddy said, but he pushed the sheet back and sat up.

Hugh rushed over to the window. "Hurry!"

His father seemed to be taking forever. By the time he got to the window, Hugh was looking wildly up and down the beach for the periscope. It was gone.

"Where is it, Hugh?" Daddy said. "I don't see a thing."

"It's gone now…but it was out there, I know it was!" Tears were stinging his eyes.

"Hugh." In the moonlight Hugh could see his father shaking his head.

"It *was* out there," he said again. "I saw it."

"You must have been dreaming," Daddy said. He took Hugh by his shoulders and walked him back to his room. "Get some sleep," he said. He pulled the sheet up and kissed Hugh on the forehead. "God bless."

Just before the door to their room closed Hugh heard his

mother say, "Maybe you'd better have a talk with Hugh while you're here. He's obsessed with all this war stuff. When he's not lying on a sand dune staring through those binoculars, he's shut up in his room fooling with that scrapbook."

Hugh sighed. After a few minutes he got out of bed and went back to the window. He stood there a long time, hoping to see the sub again. But all he saw was the moonlight on the water. And then some clouds drifted in front of the moon, and everything was dark.

Chapter Five

It was late when Hugh woke up the next morning. He went to the front window and looked out. A few people were already on the beach, swimming or lying in the sun. A man was surf casting. Hugh wanted to shout to them, "Watch out! It's not safe!" He sighed and shook his head. They wouldn't believe him, either.

When he got downstairs his mother was on the front porch looking through the binoculars. Hugh shaded his eyes with his hand and saw a big clump of people up the beach.

"Good morning," Mama said, handing him the binoculars. "Want to see? The German prisoners of war are taking a swim."

When Hugh and his family had come up to the beach from Charleston in early June, they'd driven past some men in blue shirts and pants who were working in a swampy area near the roadside. White letters—POW—were stenciled on the backs of their shirts and the seats of their pants.

Hugh and Sally were in the backseat. "What's 'pow'?" Sally asked. She made it rhyme with "now."

Daddy slowed up just a little. "P-O-W," he said. "Prisoner of war."

Hugh felt a thrill of excitement. "Germans?"

"Yes," his father said, "captured in North Africa."

"The Afrika Korps!" Hugh said. "General Rommel was their commander. The Desert Fox. And they had all those tanks—they're called *Panzers* in German. And the British stopped them at El Alamein."

"Oh, Hugh, you think you know everything," Sally said.

He stuck his tongue out at her and she jabbed him in the ribs with her elbow.

"But why are those men here?" Hugh said.

"There wasn't room for them in the prison camps in North Africa," Daddy said, "so they were sent to the United States and put to work. Farm work, mostly. Clearing swamps. There's a camp not far from here, up near Myrtle Beach."

Hugh turned around and knelt on the seat, looking back at the prisoners. And then he realized American soldiers were standing at intervals along the side of the road. They had rifles. He kept his eyes glued on the soldiers until the car went around a curve and they were out of sight.

Now, looking through the binoculars, he could see there were soldiers with rifles on the beach, too. "What if a German tries to swim away?" he asked his mother. "Isn't it their duty to escape?"

She laughed. "If they wanted to escape, that's the only way they could go," she said, pointing at the horizon. "They'd have to swim clear back to North Africa."

What a dumb question. Hugh wished he hadn't asked it. Still, if one of them was a good enough swimmer, couldn't he swim underwater, far enough away…

20

Mama squeezed the back of his neck. "You don't need to worry about them escaping," she said. "They'd probably much rather be here than in Russia, getting killed."

"I'm not worried," Hugh muttered. "But they—"

"Look," Mama said. "Daddy and Abram." She pointed straight out to sea, beyond the breakers, to a boat with two tiny figures in it.

Hugh trained the binoculars on the boat. "They're a long way out," he said. And then he caught his breath. The sub— it could be out there. It could be right under the boat... But no. That couldn't happen. Daddy and Abram were bottom-fishing, which meant the water wasn't all that deep. Much too shallow for a sub.

Or was it? The periscope last night—it had seemed so close.

"Abram swore there's a huge school of whiting just wait-ing for them out there," Mama was saying. "It must've been four-thirty when Daddy got up to go." She yawned. "I'd go back to bed if it wasn't so hot."

But it wasn't the fishermen Hugh was interested in. It was the men up the beach. He was turning to look at them again when his mother said, "Run on inside and get some breakfast. Mattie's waited for you long enough."

Hugh started to protest, but then he remembered what he'd heard his mother say to his father the night before. Maybe he shouldn't show too much excitement about the POWs. He went inside, sat at the kitchen table, and started eating almost before Mattie had finished putting his plate down in front of him. She shook her head.

"Hugh, you're eating so fast, that food's gonna sit on your stomach like a rock," she said. Mattie was Abram's wife. She'd been cooking for their family every summer since Hugh's father was a boy.

Hugh didn't pay her any attention. She was always saying stuff like that. All he could think about was the German prisoners. The Enemy. He needed to see them up close, before they were taken back to the camp.

As he went upstairs to brush his teeth, Sally came out of her room. She had on her bathing suit. "Coming out on the beach?" she asked.

"In a little while." He brushed his teeth, put on his tennis shoes, and went back downstairs. His mother was in the living room reading the newspaper. Without making a sound, Hugh took the binoculars off the hat rack and hung them around his neck. He peered into the kitchen. Mattie was right there, doing something at the sink. She didn't even look up when he slipped out the back door.

Hugh jogged along the winding creek road until he saw two U.S. Army trucks, the kind with open backs and benches along the sides for troops to sit on. They were parked in a sandy area next to a thicket of low-growing myrtle trees. A driveway led through the trees toward an old deserted house and an open stretch of beach.

He checked to be sure no one was around, then turned into the driveway. The weeds were waist-high except where they'd been beaten down by the prisoners and their guards on their way up to the beach. Hugh pretended he didn't see the No Trespassing sign nailed to a palmetto tree. He followed the curve of the driveway until the old house came into view. It sat up high off the ground, just like their house did. It looked as lonely as ever. Most of the green shingles were missing from the roof. The sagging porch that ran all the way around the house looked as if it might fall off any minute. In the upstairs windows, broken shades hung at crazy angles. This was the first time Hugh had seen it from the back. He and Sally called it the Spook House.

He climbed the steps to the porch and started around to the front of the house. The porch floor slanted so much he had to reach out now and then and steady himself on the wobbly railing. About halfway around, he almost fell into a charred hole. It looked as if somebody had built a fire right there on the porch and it had burned all the way through. Probably a bum. Or maybe some hoodlums from over on the mainland having a party.

Hugh crept around the hole, rounded the corner, and stopped. He caught his breath. There, out on the beach on the other side of the dunes, were the German POWs.

He wiped his face on his shirtsleeve. Leaning up against the wall of the house, he trained his binoculars on the men. As far as he could tell they looked just like Americans, nothing like the Germans' allies, the Japanese. Hugh remembered an article that had come out in *TIME* magazine right after war was declared—"How to Tell Your Friends from the Japs." There were pictures of four men, two Chinese, two Japanese. He had studied them for a long time. Since then he'd seen lots of pictures of General Tojo, the Japanese commander-in-chief, who wore round, black-rimmed glasses and had a mustache and snaggle-teeth, but he still wasn't sure he could tell Japanese and Chinese apart. He wondered if it was the same for them.

The German prisoners looked just like men on the street back in Charleston. Hugh shivered. He could walk right past one of them and not even know he was an enemy.

Not long ago, at the movies, he'd seen an old newsreel of a Nazi Party rally in Nuremberg, Germany. It was back in 1938, just before the war started. There were thousands and thousands of people, bands playing marches, and about a million flags with swastikas on them. Hitler was up on this huge reviewing stand with his black hair pasted down on his forehead and that funny-looking mustache sprouting out from under his big old nose. A formation of boys in shorts and long socks came goose-stepping past him— "Hitler Youth." They threw up their right arms and shouted, *"Heil Hitler!"* Hitler raised his arm at the elbow and flapped his hand at them.

Those boys hadn't looked much older than Hugh was now. Twelve, thirteen, maybe. Tom's age. Would he and Tom have been in the Hitler Youth if they were Germans? Tom probably would be—he was big and blond. He'd be shaving soon—he had a razor. Hugh adjusted the binoculars. The prisoners out there on the beach didn't look like *they'd* ever been in the Hitler Youth. They were wearing their white undershorts for bathing suits, and their bodies were white, too, except for their sunburned faces and necks and hands. Not all of them were swimming. A few men were sitting at the edge of the water, playing in the sand like children.

The guards were standing around, smoking, talking to each other, laughing. Then suddenly one of them blew a whistle and ran down toward the edge of the water. He shouted, signaling to a prisoner who'd swum out a long way past the others. The guard shouted again, and the man out in the water yelled something back and started swimming in toward the beach. He was a good swimmer. When he got close in, he stood up. He was big and strong looking. He stood there in the surf, his hands on his hips, looking in toward land, toward the Spook House. Hugh felt a prickle of fear. He knew the man couldn't see him, but still, what was he looking at?

There was a noise close by. Hugh froze. Was it footsteps? Heavy breathing? But then he relaxed. It was Jiggs, trotting around the side of the porch, panting like a steam engine.

"I might've known you'd find me," Hugh whispered. "But you'd better be quiet, hear?"

That seemed to suit Jiggs just fine. He lay down and closed his eyes.

Hugh shrugged to loosen up his shoulders and felt a sharp pain. A splinter from the wall had needled into his back. Just then the whistle blew again. Jiggs raised his head. "Shhh," Hugh whispered.

The guards were beginning to round up the POWs. Hugh lifted the binoculars to his eyes one last time. The big man was still standing there looking straight at the Spook House. When a guard yelled at him, the man walked slowly through the water up onto the beach. He picked up a towel and dried off, then stood by himself, away from the others.

Hugh waited until the prisoners began to line up in formation, and then he edged around the corner of the porch and headed for home with Jiggs loping along beside him.

Chapter Six

B e still, Hugh!"

"It hurts, Mattie!"

He was sitting on the kitchen stool while Mattie dug at the splinter in his back with a needle she'd sterilized with a lit match. When she'd asked how he got the splinter, he'd said he had no idea.

There was another prick, and then Mattie said, "Got it!" She reached around and held the splinter up in front of him. "Teeny little thing," she said.

"Well, it still hurt," he said, and started to get up.

Mattie pushed him back down and came around and looked him in the eyes. "What are you up to, Hughboy?" she said. "I saw you slip out of this house with those spyglasses round your neck. Old Mattie's got eyes in the back of her head."

"Birdwatching," he said. "There's a nest of baby herons in the marsh just up the road."

"Since when are you a birdwatcher, Hugh?" she said.

"For ages. I do it all the time in Charleston."

"All the time," she said. "Un-hunh. I bet." She gave him a little push. "Go on. The rest of them are out on the beach. Don't you go upstairs and stick your nose in that scrapbook. Go play."

He stopped on the porch on his way out and looked up the beach just in case. The prisoners were gone.

* * *

Hugh sat on the bench out on the dock, watching Daddy and Abram clean fish. They'd had a huge catch, not just whiting, but blackfish, too.

"Well, that's about it," Daddy said. He held out a tin basin full of cleaned fish. "Hugh, think you can eat a few of these?"

"Yes sir!" Just thinking about how good they were going to taste after Mattie had fried them made Hugh's mouth water.

Daddy washed his hands and arms in a bucket of water Hugh had brought from the house. Abram wrapped the fish scales and entrails in old newspapers. The fish heads went into a paper bag. He would use them for crab bait.

Daddy sat down next to Hugh. He lit a cigarette and blew out a plume of smoke. "Wonderful morning, Abram," he said. "Wonderful. Just what I needed."

"I'm glad," Abram said. He lit a cigarette, too, and sat down on the opposite bench.

"I've told you this before, Abram," Daddy said, "but I'll say it again. I can't tell you how much I'm counting on you to look out for things around here. All these women and children…"

Abram chuckled. "'All these women and children.' Not so many."

"Well…enough," Daddy said. He sighed and shook his head. "I wish I could be as calm, cool, and collected as you, Abram."

Abram frowned. "Calm, cool, and what?"

"Collected."

Abram chuckled again and tapped his midsection with his knuckle. "Churning in here sometimes," he said.

Daddy tapped his own midsection. "Churning in here almost all the time."

Hugh frowned. *Churning?* Was Daddy worried about something going on in Charleston? Something he knew about because of his Civil Defense job? Something he couldn't tell them about? Hugh got so tired of hearing his friends at school brag about what their fathers were doing—one was in England with the Army and another one on a ship in the Pacific. But maybe—his heart gave a thump—maybe Daddy was doing something even more dangerous…

His father stood up. "I would never leave my family here if you and Mattie weren't around to look after them."

Abram looked over at Hugh and nodded. Then he looked back at Daddy. "It is my honor," he said.

When they all got back to the house, Abram set up the stepladder at the top of the stairs and installed a blackout lamp Daddy had ordered from a store in New York. That night, when they were all getting ready to go upstairs to bed, he turned off the downstairs lights and switched on the blackout lamp. It cast a strange soft blue light.

"Gracious," Mama said, "I don't know whether I like that thing or not."

Daddy put his arm around her. "Well, my dear," he said, "at least now you and the children won't fall down and break your crowns. You can leave it on all night. And not a soul outside this house will see it."

* * *

Before Daddy left that evening, he and Hugh went for a walk on the beach. The sun was already low in the sky, its long rays slanting just over the rooftops of the houses behind the dunes.

Daddy stopped and touched Hugh on the shoulder. "Look at the color of that water out there," he said. "It's almost purple. With gold stripes from the sun. Beautiful, isn't it?"

Hugh nodded. "Yes sir."

"We're lucky to be here, aren't we?" Daddy said. "To have this place." His voice sounded a little shaky.

Hugh became very busy digging a hole in the sand with his big toe. In a minute he stole a look at his father. He was standing with his arms folded, looking out to sea. Hugh wondered again why when they were out on the dock yesterday he had told Abram he was "churning" inside. Was it the war? Or was he afraid of something else?

Hugh took a deep breath. "Daddy," he said, "could a submarine come in close along here?" But his father turned away and whistled for Jiggs. Hugh went around to his other side, to his good ear.

"Daddy! Could a sub come in close along here?" he said again.

Daddy leaned down and raised his eyebrows. "A submarine? Well, I don't know—fairly close, maybe. But I seriously doubt it. Why?" But then he shook his head, remembering. "Oh, that periscope you thought you saw—"

"But I did—"

Daddy knelt down on the sand and put his hand on Hugh's shoulders. "Look at me, son," he said. "Maybe you'd better lighten up on all the war stuff. Mama's a little worried about you. Can't you find things to do with Sally and Tom?"

Hugh ducked his head and jammed his hands into his pockets.

"Hugh?"

He looked back at his father. "I saw a periscope! I know I did!" He was shouting. He couldn't help it.

Daddy stood up. "All right, all right," he said. "I'll tell you what. You keep a log of what you find and what you...ah...you see. Then the next time I'm here, we'll go over it together, okay?"

"But Daddy—"

"If you see anything else that's really suspicious, you tell your mother, and she can get in touch with the...um... proper authorities."

"Jack!" It was Mama, coming up the beach. "It'll be dark before long. You'd better get a move on."

After Daddy left, Hugh went upstairs to his room. He got out his scrapbook and turned to an empty page in back. At the top of the page he wrote the word LOG.

Below that he started his list.

1. Friday—1st sighting of periscope
2. Saturday—cigarette package
3. Saturday night—2nd sighting of periscope

He stared at what he'd written. It sure didn't look like much. He sighed and put his pencil down.

Later he sat out on the back steps for a while, watching the huge red sun go down. He saw the osprey heading for its nest in a dead tree across the marsh, and then a man paddling along in a skiff. There was a flash, and, like a rock, the sun sank below the trees over on the mainland. Behind him in the kitchen he could hear Mama humming a little tune while she fixed supper. Mattie left every day around three o'clock.

He leaned back against the screen door and closed his eyes. "Can't you find things to do with Sally and Tom?" Daddy had said. But he didn't *want* to do things with his sister and Tom all the time. It wasn't much fun because Sally thought Tom was so great.

And *Tom* thought Tom was so great.

Anyway, he needed some time alone, time to think about things. Especially when there was so much to think about.

Chapter Seven

A storm blew in the next morning. The sky was an ugly yellow-tinged gray. The wind was howling, kicking up the surf so it was much too rough for swimming. All day Sally and the boys had been stuck inside, reading, working puzzles, playing games.

"I'm bored," Sally said for the one-millionth time. It was about three in the afternoon and they were playing Monopoly. Hugh had hotels on Park Place and Boardwalk, and Tom owned all the utilities.

"We just have to wait it out," Mama said. She was on the sofa across the room, reading. "It'll probably blow itself out by tomorrow."

"It already seems like a month," Sally said. "What can we do? I'm sick of Monopoly."

"That's because you always lose," Hugh said. "You think you have to buy every property you land on."

Tom laughed.

"Shut up, Hugh." Sally pushed away from the table and went over to her mother. "Mama..."

Mama sighed and put her book down. "Please don't whine," she said. She put her arm around Sally's waist. "Why don't you write Granny a letter? She'd love to hear from you. Or one of your friends—"

"I don't want to!" Sally broke away and went out on the porch, letting the screen door slam behind her. Mama sighed again and went back to her book.

"Your move, Hugh," Tom said.

In just a few minutes Sally was back. She leaned over and whispered in Hugh's ear, "Let's show Tom the Spook House."

Hugh gave her a quick look, and then he shook his head.

"Why not?" she said.

"Because..."

The Spook House had been their special place, his and Sally's, ever since they were little, even though they'd never even been inside. They'd made up all sorts of stories about it—that it was a pirates' hideout, or that there was a Yankee soldier's skeleton lying in an upstairs bedroom. Or that sometimes, if the light was right, you could see a face up in the cupola.

But now he *had* been up close to it, closer than Sally could imagine...

"Hugh!" Sally put her hands on her hips. "Because *why? Why* can't we go?"

He looked over at their mother. She was reading again. "Because," he whispered, "Mama and Daddy said to stay away from—"

She gave him a little shove. "They don't have to know."

Tom was looking at them, his eyebrows raised.

Sally walked over to Mama. "We're going to play under the house, okay?"

Mama was half-asleep. "It's mighty windy," she murmured. "Be careful…and watch out for the ants." She closed her eyes and put her book down on her chest.

"What's going on?" Tom said.

"Come on, we'll show you," Sally said, and she went outside, making sure the screen door didn't slam this time. Tom was right behind her.

Hugh sat at the card table counting his Monopoly money—more than three thousand dollars, at least twice as much as Tom. He tucked his bills under the Monopoly board, and then he got up and stood at the door to the porch, looking out at the gray ocean. "Oh, what the heck," he muttered, and pushed the door open.

Sally and Tom were sitting on the bench outside the shower room. She was telling him about the Spook House. "It's been empty for years and years."

Hugh stood apart from them, looking out at the ocean. The wind blew sand through the open spaces in the latticework that ran around the bottom of the house. He stepped back.

"The family who owns it—they didn't get along with each other," Sally said, "and they couldn't agree on who was in charge of keeping the house up, so *nobody* kept it up. Now it just sits there, rotting away. They probably could've rented it for a lot of money. Isn't that right, Hugh?"

Hugh turned around and shrugged.

"Well, they could. It's huge," she said. "But now..." She shook her head.

"What's so special about it?" Tom said.

Sally looked at Hugh again. He shrugged again. "I don't know, it's—it's spooky!" Sally said. "And at least it's something to do. Come on, let's go."

They went by the beach. It was quicker that way. The way Hugh had gone the other morning—the road along the creek—took much longer because of all the curves. Jiggs followed them a little way, but then he gave up and trotted back toward the house. The wind came whistling straight down the beach, right into their faces. The boys pulled their shirttails up over their faces to keep the sand out of their eyes. Sally turned around and walked backwards. She could go almost as fast backwards as Hugh could go forward.

Hugh was counting the houses between their house and the Spook House. He'd gotten to eight when Sally pointed up over the dunes. "There it is," she said. From here they could just see the long green roof with chimneys at either end and the little cupola right in the middle. A tall palmetto tree on one side swayed in the wind. They climbed up to the top of a sand dune and stood looking at the house. It was much farther back from the beach than Hugh remembered from the other day. But he'd had the binoculars then, and things had seemed closer, much closer.

Sally stood there, the sea oats whipping at her legs, the wind blowing her blond hair around her face.

"Well, let's go check out the big scary Spook House," Tom said. He made it all sound so silly. So babyish.

"Why don't you just go on back to our house, Tom?" Hugh said.

But Tom didn't even look at him. He started walking down the dune toward the house. Sally hesitated, and then she dashed after him.

The remains of an old boardwalk ran across the sand through clumps of sea oats and spiky Spanish bayonets. It ended right in front of the house, where the front steps used to be. Nothing was there now but a black space, like a giant missing tooth.

Halfway down the boardwalk Sally turned around and looked back. "Come on, Hugh!" she shouted. "What's the matter? Are you afraid?"

That's all it took. In a few seconds Hugh was standing with her and Tom at the end of the boardwalk.

Chapter Eight

The house loomed up over them. "What about that?" Tom said. He was pointing at a No Trespassing sign nailed to the porch railing. Hugh hadn't even noticed it, but he remembered the one on the driveway the other day—the one he'd pretended not to see.

"What about it?" Sally said.

"We're trespassing," Tom said. "We could get arrested."

"Who's going to catch us?" Sally said. "There isn't a single policeman on this whole island. They're all over in Georgetown. They hardly ever come over here." Georgetown was thirteen miles away.

"Let's try the back," Hugh said. "We can't get up there this way." He led them around the side of the house, but when he got to the back steps, Sally pushed in front of him. He shook his head. She just *had* to be first.

She and Tom ran along the side porch. Suddenly Hugh remembered the hole in the floor. "Hey!" he yelled. "Watch out for the—"

But they'd seen it and stopped in time. Sally was peering down into the hole. "Too dark to see anything," she said, "but I bet there's plenty of good stuff down there."

"Like what?" Tom said.

"Oh, I don't know," Sally said. "Just stuff."

"Beer bottles, probably," Hugh said.

Sally straightened up and went over to a window. She cupped her hands over her eyes. "Can't see a thing," she said. She licked her finger, rubbed a little circle on the glass, and looked again.

"There's still some furniture in there," she said. "I thought it was empty." She wiped her hand on her shorts.

Tom was at the front door, yanking hard at the handle. He shook his head and held up his hands. They were orange with rust.

They worked their way around the porch from window to window, checking the locks, looking for promising cracks. No luck. At the back of the house a section of the porch had been screened in. Now the screening hung in shreds that waved in the wind like Spanish moss. An almost-bald mop was propped against the wall, next to a door. A huge pot with a rusted-out bottom sat on the floor.

"The kitchen must be in here," Sally said. She turned the knob, pushed, and with a screech, the door opened. "Bingo!" she said.

"Careful—" Hugh began, but Sally and Tom were already inside. Hugh went to the edge of the porch and looked out toward the driveway. No sign of anybody, no sound of cars out on the road. He turned back and went inside.

It was a big, old-fashioned kitchen with a huge sink, a little refrigerator on legs, and an old black woodstove squatting next to an electric stove. Sally prowled around the room, opening and closing cabinets and drawers, turning the knobs on the stove, wrestling with the faucets over the sink. "There's no water or electricity," she announced.

"Surprise, surprise," Hugh said.

They went into the dining room. A few broken chairs were scattered around a long, dusty table. Draped across one wall was a ragged fishing net decorated with shells— sand dollars, conchs, a still-beautiful starfish. A high chair covered with cobwebs stood in a corner.

The living room stretched all the way across the front of the house. In front of the fireplace was a huge sofa that had lost most of its insides. A faded deck of cards, curly at the edges, and a stack of poker chips sat on a rickety table surrounded by chairs. The room was dark and smelled of mice and mildew. Everything was covered with dust and a fine coating of sand.

There were two bare bedrooms and a bath downstairs, and upstairs, more bedrooms and baths. The only furniture they saw on the second floor was in a long room at the back, where three steel double-deckers were lined up against one wall, their mattresses black with mildew. No skeletons of Yankee soldiers anywhere.

"Pee-ew!" Sally said, making a face. "It stinks in here." A gust of wind slapped the fronds of the palmetto tree against the windowpanes. "Let's go," she said. "I don't like this place. It's *too* spooky."

She and Tom headed back down the hallway. Hugh started after them, but then he stopped. There was a ladder attached to the wall. He looked up and saw a square trapdoor in the ceiling. As soon as Tom and Sally disappeared down the stairs, he jumped up and grabbed the lowest rung of the ladder. He pulled himself up and got a foothold. The ladder swayed a little, and then steadied. He climbed up, checking each rung before putting his weight on it.

At the top, he saw that only a lightweight piece of plywood covered the opening. He pushed it aside and hoisted himself up. He was in the cupola they'd seen from the beach. It was like a tiny room with windows all around. On all four sides were shutters missing most of their slats. The wind came whistling through the gaps so hard he almost lost his balance. Bird droppings were everywhere.

He crouched under the low ceiling and slowly turned three hundred and sixty degrees. From here he could see in every direction. Out to sea, all the way to each end of the island, back over the marsh to the mainland. Now *his* was the scary face in the cupola!

"Hugh! Hugh!" Sally called from the foot of the stairs. "You'd better come on. We're going to get in trouble—"

"Coming," he yelled. He took one more look around. Then he eased his legs through the trapdoor and started back down the ladder.

Chapter Nine

Hugh sat in the armchair next to the radio. Mama was up the beach visiting her friend Mrs. Collins. The evening news was just coming on. The announcer began: "Here with a keen analysis of the news—"

Blam! The screen door slammed. Sally and Tom came in off the porch. "Listen!" Sally said. "It's good old H. V. Kaltenborn."

"Who's he?" Tom asked.

"Hugh's favorite person. He! Talks! Just! Like! This!" She imitated the newscaster's staccato delivery.

"Shut up, Sally!" Hugh yelled. "I'm trying to listen to the news!"

But she didn't shut up. She strutted around the room chanting "H. V. Kal-ten-born! H. V. Kal-ten-born!"

Tom was laughing his head off, and then he started doing it, too, marching after Sally, chanting "H. V. Kal-ten-born!" They threw their arms up in the Nazi salute.

"Are you crazy?" Hugh screamed. "He's not a Nazi!" But they weren't paying one bit of attention to him. Hugh turned up the volume and pressed his ear against the radio.

Finally Tom and Sally stopped marching and collapsed onto the sofa. They were still giggling, acting like four year olds.

Hugh turned off the radio and waited until they quieted down. Then he said, "You know what?"

"*What*, Hugh?" Sally said.

"You might not be laughing so much if you'd heard what he—Mr. Kaltenborn—was saying."

"What?" Tom still had a smirk on his face.

"Two more of our ships were sunk today. In the Atlantic. No survivors."

"Oh," Sally said. She frowned at him and shook her head. Then she went over to the card table and started fooling with the dice from the Monopoly game.

But Tom just sat there, his head bowed. Then he took a deep breath and got up. He walked across the room, edged around the card table, and went upstairs. They heard his door close.

Hugh turned the radio back on. The newscast was over.

* * *

Something woke Hugh in the middle of the night—people talking. He got out of bed. Across the hall, Mama's light was on. He tiptoed down to Sally's room and peeked in. She was asleep. But light showed around the closed door to Tom's room. Hugh moved closer and heard his mother's low voice. Then he heard Tom. It sounded like he was crying.

Tom, crying?

Hugh slipped back into his room, got into bed, and put a pillow over his head.

The Coastwatcher

* * *

When Hugh woke up the next morning, the sun was out. He sniffed. No smell of anything cooking, so Mattie must not be here. That meant it wasn't seven-thirty yet.

He got dressed and went downstairs. Nobody else was up. He was just taking the binoculars off the hat rack when he heard the jingle of Jiggs's tags.

"Want to go with me, boy?" he said. Jiggs sat down and scratched himself. Then he padded over and stood by the front door.

They went out on the porch. The ocean was as calm as a lake. Not a single fisherman out, no birds except for a line of pelicans cruising along in the light southwesterly breeze.

Jiggs waited at the bottom of the steps until Hugh came down, then trotted after him. They crossed the dunes and headed up the beach. Jiggs ran ahead, zigging and zagging. Every few yards he stopped to sniff at something interesting.

"You're up early, Hugh!"

He jumped. It was Mrs. Collins, Mama and Daddy's friend, standing up on her porch in a pink bathrobe, a coffee cup in her hand. Her long, peroxide-blond hair was tied up in turkeytails that waggled when she moved her head. She was the only divorced person Hugh knew. And she'd been divorced *twice*.

"See anything?" she called. She put her cup down and curled her hands in front of her eyes like she was looking through binoculars.

He reached up and touched the binoculars around his neck, and then he grinned and shook his head.

"Tell your mother to call me. I'm going into Georgetown this morning if she wants to go with me."

"Yes ma'am."

She gave a lazy wave and turned to go inside. Hugh broke into a jog. When he got close to the Spook House, he climbed up over the dune, sat down, and raised the binoculars to his eyes.

Even in the bright sunlight the house looked sinister. For the first time he noticed how vines grew up and into the chimneys, how low the wooden awnings came down over the upper windows. There was a heaviness about it, a stillness, as if—he squeezed his eyes shut, trying to think of the word—as if it was brooding. That was it, brooding.

He thought again of the man on the beach, the prisoner of war. What was he looking for the other day when he'd stood in the surf, staring up at the house? He couldn't have seen Hugh—the porch roof sagged down so far everything under it was in shadow. He'd just stood there apart from all the others, staring at the Spook House. And none of them had come near him.

Down the beach the breakfast bell at the inn two doors from their house clanged. Eight-fifteen. Time to go back. But Hugh didn't want to. There was something about the Spook House that drew him...

Jiggs whined and pawed at Hugh's arm. *He* was hungry, even if Hugh wasn't.

Hugh stood up and brushed the sand off his shorts. "Okay, let's go."

On the way back home, he stopped for a moment. The osprey was out there just beyond the breakers hunting for its breakfast, its wings beating and beating. And then, so fast Hugh could hardly see it, down it plunged, feet first. There was a little splash and the osprey swooped up, a fish wriggling in its claws. Hugh smiled. They weren't called "fish hawks" for nothing. If he were a bird, he'd want to be an osprey.

When he got home, Mama was standing out on the porch. "Hurry up!" she called. "You know how it upsets Mattie when we're late for meals."

"Took Jiggs for a walk," Hugh mumbled as he hung the binoculars back up. "I saw Mrs. Collins. She said to tell you she was going in to Georgetown this morning."

"Thank you. I'll call her after breakfast."

Hugh followed Mama into the dining room and slipped into his chair just as Mattie walked in from the kitchen with a platter of bacon and eggs. "I saw the osprey," he said. "He caught a giant fish."

"Hmph," Mattie grunted. "Osprey. Mr. Hugh Birdwatcher. Hmph." On her way back to the kitchen she managed to give his chair a bump with her large hip.

Sally giggled. "Good going, Hugh." She looked over at Tom. "H. V. Kal-ten-born," she whispered, but Tom looked away.

Suddenly Hugh remembered last night, Tom crying. Now Mama was chattering away, trying to get Tom to talk, but he ate just a few bites of his breakfast and then asked to be excused. He got up from the table and went upstairs.

"What's the matter with *him?*" Sally said.

"Maybe you two can tell *me,*" Mama said. "There was something on the news—"

"Oh, about those ships being sunk," Sally said. "Tom didn't actually hear it. Hugh told him."

"You told him about the ships, Hugh?" Mama said.

"Why not?"

"Well, after all, Hugh, his father's on a ship," Mama said.

"Then Tom ought to be the one listening to the news," Hugh said, "so he'd know what's going on."

"Well, his father was *not* on one of those ships, thank goodness," Mama said. "His ship wasn't to leave Norfolk until Friday. But you need to be more careful."

"What am I supposed to do?" Hugh said. "Stop listening to the news? Stop reading this?" He held up the newspaper, which was folded next to his plate. He opened it to the front page and showed them the headline: TWO MORE SHIPS LOST IN THE ATLANTIC. "Are we supposed to pretend it's not happening?" He was almost shouting.

"Quiet down," Mama said, "and don't be silly. Try to be more considerate."

Across from him, Sally was taking tiny little bites of her scrambled eggs.

Hugh's face was burning. Considerate! How considerate were Sally and Tom when they came busting in last night while he was trying to listen to the news? All that stomping around and chanting and making fun of H. V. Kaltenborn. The Nazi salutes. "If Daddy was on a ship," he said, "I'd certainly try to keep track of—"

"Well, Daddy's not," Mama said. "And you're not Tom."

"He thinks he's so great just because his father—"

"Oh, Hugh." Mama looked tired. "It's not like you to be unkind."

"I don't know what Hugh's talking about," Sally said. "I've never heard Tom say one word about his father. Anyway, he'd probably rather be at camp than here with us."

Hugh took a deep breath. What he wanted to say was "That would be just fine with me."

But he didn't.

Chapter Ten

Hugh came in the back door. He'd been downstairs under the house, stomping on tin cans to flatten them. Everyone was supposed to save anything that would go toward the "war effort." Hugh and Sally collected tin cans, old pots and pans, and anything rubber— old hoses and tennis shoes and tires. Mama's worn-out nylon stockings. Newspapers. Even empty toothpaste tubes and chewing gum wrappers. Their school occasionally had "scrap drives," and the student who contributed the most stuff won five dollars.

Mattie was standing at the kitchen counter, staring down at something in a big blue bowl.

"What's that, Mattie?" Hugh said. She moved aside so he could look in the bowl. There was a rectangular white blob with some orange stuff sprinkled on top of it. "Oh," he said, "you're going to make some butter."

"Butter! What you mean, butter? How do they expect me to cook with this mess? Nothing but a big hunk of...of lard and Easter-egg dye." She took a big wooden spoon and began beating the stuff in the bowl like it was a deadly enemy. "This rationing! Can't get eggs! Can't get coffee! Can't get—" She stopped and looked over at Hugh. He was grinning. She burst into laughter. "You know your old Mattie, don't you, Hugh?"

"Sure do," Hugh said. "Where's Mama?"

"Out on the porch," Mattie said. "But don't you go bothering her, Hugh."

Hugh's heart gave a thump. "What's wrong?"

"Your mama's feeling sad. I think it was something in that letter she got this morning."

Hugh went out onto the porch. He could see Sally and Tom on the beach, playing rollerbat with some children who were staying down at the inn. As usual, Tom was the batter.

Mama was sitting in a rocking chair at the end of the porch. He walked down and sat on the railing, facing her. "Hey," she said. A blue envelope was lying in her lap. "Don't you want to go play rollerbat?"

He shook his head. "It's no fun anymore."

"What do you mean 'anymore'?"

"Tom hits the ball so hard nobody can get him out, so nobody else gets to be the batter."

Mama sighed and shook her head. She didn't seem to have heard a word he said. "Sometimes life's not fair," she said.

"Who's the letter from?" Hugh said.

She looked down at the envelope in her lap. "Caroline," she said. "She's having such a tough time." Caroline was Mama's college roommate. She lived up in Connecticut.

"What's wrong?"

"It's her husband. He's Jewish. He has family in Europe and he's terribly worried about what's happening over there."

Hugh frowned. "You mean the war?"

"Not just that. About what's happening to the Jews."

"What's happening to them?"

"People are saying that the Nazis have been rounding up Jewish people all over Europe and making them live in these camps—"

"Rounding them up? What do you mean?"

Mama paused. "Taking them from their homes, honey. Taking them all to one place."

"But why, Mama? What have they done wrong?"

"Nothing. Not a thing." Her voice quavered.

"You mean it would be like people coming here and making us leave? Making us live somewhere else?"

She nodded.

"But why hasn't it been in the newspaper or on the radio?"

"I don't know. It seems to have sneaked up on us...on America. Oh, Hugh, it's all so awful—the war—everything." She wiped her eyes with her handkerchief and took a deep breath. "At least we're safe here," she said.

Hugh swallowed. "I'm not so sure, Mama," he began, but she held out her arms.

"Come here and give me a hug," she said. He leaned over and put his arms around her and kissed the top of her head. More than anything he wanted to tell her about the periscope, the cigarette package in the crab's claw. But not right now. Not when she was so upset.

He looked out at the beach. One of the boys from the inn was batting. "Maybe I'll go play a little rollerbat after all," he said.

Chapter Eleven

Before lunch, Hugh worked on his maps with a red pencil, bringing them up to date. They were tacked along the wall next to the staircase. Red stood for the Allies—American, British, and Russian forces. Ever since mid-May and the conclusion of Operation Torch, all of French North Africa had been solid red. In a few days, all of Sicily would be that way, too. A thin brownish yellow strip running along the eastern coast of the island was all that was left of the enemy. Hugh had picked the ugliest color he could find to represent the Axis forces—the Germans and Italians.

"What's going on?" Tom asked, looking over Hugh's shoulder. It was the first time he'd shown any interest in the maps. Hugh showed him Sicily on the Mediterranean map and told him how it would be the "springboard" for invading Italy. But when he began to explain the details, he realized he was talking to himself. Tom had walked away. Hugh shook his head and went back to the map.

Sicily lay just across from the "toe" of Italy's bootlike shape, where the next invasion would come. Mussolini had already been forced to resign. Hugh had seen him on the newsreels. He was a large man who strutted around like he owned the world. He called himself *Il Duce*—the leader.

Mussolini was fat, but not as fat as Field Marshal Goering, commander of the German Air Force, the *Luftwaffe*. He weighed two hundred and seventy pounds and had fifty different uniforms and wore sixteen medals all at one time. Hugh wondered if Goering could even fit into an airplane. A bomber, maybe, but not a fighter, that was for sure. And even if he did get into one, Hugh figured it probably couldn't take off.

He moved over to his map of Eastern Europe. In June two years ago, three million German soldiers had invaded Russia in Operation Barbarossa. But now "the most powerful army ever seen" was being pushed back along a front that stretched for two thousand miles. More and more red was showing on Hugh's map.

Barbarossa. Torch. Hugh was fascinated with the names they gave to military operations. *Maybe I'll be a soldier one day*, he said to himself, *and go to West Point…*

* * *

Late that afternoon, Sally and Hugh took Tom up to the inlet at the north end of the island. Across the inlet lay Hog Island. No houses there—it was government property—just beach, scrub oaks, palmettos, and pines. Up on the mainland, across the marsh from the north end of Hog Island, lay the prison camp.

Stuff from the wrecks of the ships sunk last year was still

washing up, especially here at the inlet. Earlier in the summer, Sally and Hugh had found a few things—pieces of charred rope, part of a life preserver, a shoe—but nothing really exciting. They hadn't been back to the inlet in weeks. They weren't supposed to be here at all, especially now, when the tide was high.

"Watch this," Sally said. She threw a piece of driftwood out into the water. A second later it disappeared. For once Tom seemed excited. He walked up and down along the inlet, throwing whatever he could find into the water, watching as the current sucked it under.

Hugh knew firsthand about that current, how powerful it was. A couple of years ago, he'd gone bottom-fishing out beyond the breakers with Daddy and Abram. In the late afternoon, as they were coming back into the mouth of the inlet, a wave caught their boat and it capsized. Everything had turned out all right, but Hugh would never forget how scared he'd been, trying to fight against the surging water.

Now he saw something black floating in the water, not more than two feet away from him. It looked like a small bag of some kind. He edged forward and reached out, but just as his hand touched the bag, he lost his balance.

"Help!" he yelled as he toppled into the water. The current caught him and pulled him under and thrashed him around like he was in a washing machine. His chin scraped the bottom. He was going to drown!

But then someone grabbed his arm and pulled him out of the water, up onto the sand. He lay on his back, gasping. When he opened his eyes, Tom was standing over him.

"That was so stupid, Hugh!" Sally said. "Look at you—your chin's all bloody."

"Are you okay?" Tom asked.

Hugh sat up and wiped the water out of his eyes. He touched his stinging chin. Just a dot of blood came away on his finger. It was all he could do to look at Tom.

"You sure you're okay?" his cousin asked again.

Hugh nodded.

"What were you doing, anyway?" Sally said

"I thought I saw something—"

"Oh, you're *always* seeing something, Hugh," she said. "I'll tell you what—you'd better have a good story for why you're so wet. Mama's not going to be happy with you."

"I'll think of something," he said.

"I'm sure you will," she said. "You always do." She turned to Tom. "Hugh's a genius at making up excuses."

Tom shrugged. He picked up an oyster shell and skipped it across the water.

"Just don't tell her that we came up to the inlet," Sally said, scooping up another shell and skipping it farther than Tom's. The two of them walked along the edge of the inlet, gathering up more shells for a contest to see who could get the most skips.

Hugh stood up and shook himself like a dog. And then he remembered the black bag. It couldn't have gone far—he'd had it in his hand. He started walking along the edge of the water. In just a few minutes, he spotted the bag—in Jiggs's mouth.

"Give it here, boy," he said. Jiggs just wagged his tail. "Drop it, Jiggs! I'm not playing!" But Jiggs was. He ducked his head and pretended to drop the bag. Just as Hugh reached for it, he darted away.

"Jiggs!" Hugh started after him. Jiggs skidded to a stop. He'd spotted a fiddler crab scuttling across the sand. He dropped the bag and Hugh grabbed it.

The bag was rubber, about the size of the one Hugh kept his marbles in. It had a zipper across the top. He was just starting to unzip it when Sally shouted, "Hey, Hugh! Time to go!" He slipped the bag into the pocket of his shorts. Then he stood for a moment, looking across the inlet at Hog Island. It looked so empty. Even the wild pigs it was named for were gone. There was nothing over there at all.

Chapter Twelve

When they got home from the inlet, Hugh had his excuse ready for why he was wet. "A horsefly was biting my legs, so I went out in the water," he told Mama. "A wave—I guess I wasn't looking—knocked me down. Sorry."

Hugh looked over at Sally. She stuck out her tongue the tiniest bit. He wasn't sure, but Tom might have been trying not to smile. His lips were twitching.

"Go take off those wet clothes," Mama said. "And wash off that chin with some soap and water. And don't fool around. Come straight back down. Supper's almost ready."

Upstairs, Hugh took off his shorts and pulled the rubber bag out of the pocket. He started to unzip it, but the zipper wouldn't move.

He tried working the zipper back and forth, then pulled on it again. No luck. He gave it a good yank, so hard it hurt his hand. The zipper opened far enough for him to get two fingers inside the bag.

At first he couldn't feel anything. He forced his fingers as far down as they would go. The zipper teeth bit into his flesh. There *was* something there, something folded up. Something very soft. He eased it out. It was a piece of silk, folded up into a small square. He unfolded it and laid it on his bed. It was about the size of a dinner napkin. Gently he smoothed out the creases.

"Hugh! Supper's on the table!"

"I'm coming!" he yelled.

But he didn't take his eyes off the piece of silk. There were markings on it in indelible ink. It was a map of some sort. He could tell that much, because in one corner, there was a scale. Except instead of miles, it said "km." Hugh caught his breath. He knew what "km" stood for—kilometers. In Europe, they measured distances in kilometers, not miles.

The drawing on the silk looked like a river. Yes, that was what it must be—a river. A river that forked. Along the left bank there was a shaded area with a line of numbers running along it: 1230, 1300, 1330, 1400, 1430.

He stood there in his underwear staring down at the map, trying to figure out what it meant.

"Hugh, if you don't come right this minute—"

"Okay, okay!"

He refolded the map and tucked it and the bag under his pillow.

"I'm on my way!"

Chapter Thirteen

bram poled the boat away from the dock. A car's horn sounded, and Hugh looked up as Mrs. Collins pulled out of their driveway. She and Mama were on the way to town. Sally and Tom were going, too.

Hugh waved, and then he said, "Abram, let's go over to Hog Island."

Abram put the pole down and reached for a paddle. "What for? There's plenty crabs right here. Why you want to go all the way over yonder?"

"I want to see it," Hugh said. He cleared his throat. "Maybe we'll find something."

Abram shook his head. "What you talking about, Hugh? Ain't nothing on Hog Island. Anyway, we can't go there. Hog Island belongs to the U.S. government."

"We won't get out of the boat. Please?"

"No, Hugh." Abram paddled over to the edge of the creek. He put the paddle down and handed Hugh a crab line. "This is a good place," he said, and dropped his line over the side of the boat.

Hugh didn't move. "But Abram—"

"We'd have to go across the inlet," Abram said. "Right where that current comes in. Remember what happened that time we went with your daddy?"

For just a moment Hugh thought about the other day, how it had felt when his chin scraped against the bottom of the inlet. How he'd thought he was drowning. "I know. But it's low tide," he said. "We'll be all right. We won't be that close to the mouth of the inlet."

"Drop that line in, Hugh."

"Please. Please. There might be something over there. Something important."

Abram cocked his head and gave Hugh a hard look. "What you talking about?"

"I just have a feeling… Please, Abram. Just this once. We won't stay but a minute."

"Feeling. Boy got a feeling," Abram grumbled, but he pulled up his crab line and started paddling up toward the inlet.

The tide was dead low when they got to the inlet. They both paddled hard, and the boat skimmed across with no problems at all. As Abram paddled the boat along behind Hog Island, the creek gradually narrowed so that sometimes the grass from the marsh and the island almost met over their heads.

"I feel like Moses in the bulrushes," Abram muttered.

It was hot and very still, no breeze at all. The deerflies were biting. Abram swatted at one with his straw hat. After a while he said, "See, Hugh, nothing's over here. Wasteland. Always was. Probably ain't no crabs, either. Not along here. Let's go back."

"Just a little farther," Hugh said. "Just around that bend up there."

Abram sighed. "This is the last stretch," he said.

Around the bend the creek widened. "Okay, we're going to turn around right here," Abram said.

"Abram, look!" Hugh pointed at something up in the marsh grass.

"Where, Hugh?"

"Right there, right in front of us."

"Well, I don't see so good anymore," Abram mumbled, but he picked up his pole and started pushing the boat straight ahead.

As they drew closer, they saw a big oblong piece of gray-green rubber. It had been pushed up into the marsh—you could see where the grass was mashed down—but the tide must have moved it closer to the creek. Hugh leaned over and tried to grab it, but it was just out of his reach.

"Move, Hugh," Abram said. "Let this old man show you how to do it." He grabbed a handful of the long grass and pulled the boat as far over as it would go. Then he reached out and dragged the rubber thing halfway into the boat. For a moment they sat looking at it.

"It's a raft," Abram said. "Got a big old tear in it."

"A raft? Like they have on—on ships? On—subs?" Hugh stood up so he could see better, and the boat rocked.

"Whoa, Hugh!" Abram caught him by the arm and sat him back down. He flipped the raft over. "Looks okay on this side. Wouldn't mind having me a little boat like this. No sir, wouldn't mind a bit."

"How long you think it's been here?" Hugh said.

"Not long. Too new and shiny."

"Let's take it home," Hugh said. "You can patch it easy as anything. It'd be just like patching an inner tube, wouldn't it?"

Abram shook his head. "No sir, Hugh, can't do that. Abram's not going to get in trouble with the U.S. government. After all, we're already trespassing."

"It'll be all right, Abram," Hugh said. "They don't have to know—"

"Shame on you, Hugh," Abram said. He rolled the raft up and shoved it back into the grass. "We got to go. Tide's coming up."

Crossing the inlet, Abram had to pole hard against the incoming tide. Hugh helped out with the paddle. They were both panting by the time they got back into the channel of the creek.

"That's the last time we do *that!*" Abram said.

Hugh waited until they'd caught their breath and then he said, "Is a boat the only way to get across the inlet, Abram? Could you swim?"

"Swim?" Abram chuckled. "That's crazy, Hugh."

"But could you? Is it possible?"

"Well, maybe, but you got to be a mighty fine swimmer to do that. I reckon if you waited 'til the lowest tide, you might be able to walk some of it. Dangerous, though. Can't fool with that current."

"When does the tide get really, really low, Abram?"

"Well, you know, full moon, when the moon and the earth and the sun line up just so, and then you get real high tide and real low tide."

"When was the last full moon?"

Abram thought. "Let's see. I'd say 'bout ten days ago."

"No wait, I remember," Hugh said. "It was right after Tom got here on Thursday. It rained in the afternoon, and then it cleared up. We went swimming just before supper."

They drifted along, letting the incoming tide take them home. Every now and then Hugh gave the paddle a couple of strokes to keep them on course. Abram lit up a cigarette.

"Your hand's shaking," Hugh said.

Abram looked down at his long, wrinkled fingers. "Abram's an old man, Hugh," he said.

"You are not!" Hugh said. "You're always saying you are, but you and Daddy—"

"I'm your *granddaddy's* age, Hugh. We were boys together."

Tears welled up in Hugh's eyes. His grandfather had been dead for ages. He couldn't stand it if anything happened to Abram. He swallowed. "Abram?"

"What's that, Hugh?"

"Something's going on."

"What 'something' is going on?" Abram flicked his cigarette butt in the creek.

"I think there're Germans around here," Hugh said.

Abram took off his hat and fanned himself with it. "Lawdy, it's hot," he said. "Yep, sure are some Germans, Hugh. Right up the road, right up there on the mainland, across from Hog Island. That's no secret."

"I *know* about them, the POWs," Hugh said. "But I think...Abram, remember the other day, those cigarettes we found?"

Abram looked puzzled.

"The last time we were crabbing. Don't you remember?"

"Oh, yeah, yeah. Funny-looking package. Big ole crab had it."

"Right. Well, they're German cigarettes!"

There was a thud. Hugh grabbed the side of the boat to keep from sliding off his seat. They'd run into the bank.

"Gimme that paddle," Abram said. "You going to get us stuck." He pushed them away from the bank and back out into the creek. Hugh could see their dock now, up ahead.

"Abram, listen. It's not just the cigarettes. What about that raft—it could be a German raft, right?"

Abram shrugged. "I reckon it could."

"And the other day, I found something else. A kind of map."

"Map?" For the first time, Abram looked interested. "Where'd you find it?"

"At the inlet. Not far from where we just were. I was up there with Tom and Sally. It was in the water, in a little black rubber bag with a zipper. I had to get it away from Jiggs."

"What kind of map?" Abram asked.

"I don't know. It looked like there was a river, or a harbor, maybe."

"You show it to anybody?"

"No."

Abram didn't say anything for a few minutes, just sat staring out at a great white egret flapping along over the marsh. He took his cigarettes out of his shirt pocket, pulled one out of the package, and put it in his mouth. He rooted around in his pocket until he found a wooden kitchen match. He flicked the match with his thumbnail and lit his cigarette.

"Abram!" Sometimes Abram almost ran Hugh crazy, he was so slow.

Abram took a deep drag and watched the egret. Hugh waited as long as he could stand it. "Well, what do you think?" he asked.

Abram picked a fleck of tobacco off his bottom lip. "I think I'd like to see that map," he said, nodding. "You know what, Hugh? You may be right. Maybe there is something funny going on around here."

Hugh caught his breath. "What? Do you know about something else? Tell me!"

Abram took a deep drag off his cigarette and let the smoke drift ever so slowly out of his mouth. Hugh sighed, but something told him that it was worth waiting.

"You know Henry," Abram said.

"Sure," Hugh said. "The vegetable man." Henry came around two or three times a week, selling fresh vegetables and fruit off the back of his pickup truck.

"Well," Abram said, "Henry told me that he was up by Mrs. Collins's house, up at her back door with some field peas. Left his truck down on the road. And, you know, you can't see the road from there. Well, when he got back to the truck all his tomatoes and cantaloupes were gone. Gone! Whoever it was even took some old no-count potatoes."

"Abram! Maybe the Germans—"

"Don't know, Hugh." Abram stroked his whiskery chin and frowned. "They keep a pretty close watch on those prisoners. I haven't heard anything about any of them getting loose. Maybe we better talk to your daddy about all this."

"No!" Hugh said, so loudly Abram's head jerked up. He raised his eyebrows.

"I—I just need to be sure," Hugh said. "So if I'm wrong—"

"I see," Abram said. "You don't want nobody to tease you."

Hugh looked away. "Anyway, Daddy went back to Charleston Sunday afternoon."

"That's right. Old Abram forgets sometimes." They'd reached the dock. "Hop out, Hugh," he said. "Got to go catch me some crabs."

Hugh was climbing up the ladder onto the dock when he looked back. "Abram," he called over his shoulder. "One more thing. I saw a periscope. Twice."

Abram cupped his hand around his ear. "What's that, Hugh?"

Hugh's heart was beating like a drum. "A periscope! Like on a submarine. I saw one out in the ocean, twice!"

Abram nodded. "Is that a fact? Well, okay then, Hugh. I'll ask around. See what I can find out."

"But don't tell anyone about the map and the other stuff, okay? Not yet, anyway."

"You be careful now, Hugh. See you later." He waved a little good-bye and pushed off.

When Hugh went inside the house, nobody was there but Mattie. He ran up to his room and opened his scrapbook to the page with the log on it. He picked up his pencil and added three items to his list.

4. Wednesday—black bag with map
5. Wednesday—stolen vegetables
6. Thursday—raft

He sat on the side of his bed, looking down at the log. Should he show it to Mama? Was it time for her to go to the "proper authorities?"

Chapter Fourteen

Hugh sat looking down at his plate. The vegetables—butter beans, potatoes, and squash casserole—were fine, because Mattie was a wonderful cook. It was the SPAM. Not even Mattie could do much to make it taste better.

"What's wrong, Hugh?" his mother said. "Why aren't you eating?"

"Roast beef," he muttered.

"What?"

"I just wish we had some roast beef, that's all."

"Oh, for heaven's sake, Hugh," Mama said. "Just think how lucky we are to have fresh fish and fresh vegetables. You shouldn't complain—"

"When people overseas are starving and everything's rationed," he said. "I know, I know." He took a tiny bite of SPAM. It tasted exactly like—SPAM. All kinds of strange meats ground up and smushed into a rectangle.

"Sally, you're not eating, either," Mama said. Sally always ate everything. Even chicken livers.

"I guess I'm just not hungry," she said. Mama frowned.

Then she got up and put her hand on Sally's forehead. Sally pushed it away. "I'm all *right*, Mama," she said. "I'm just not hungry."

Sally saw Hugh looking at her. He raised his eyebrows. She shrugged.

That night Sally went upstairs before anybody else. It was the first time all summer she hadn't argued when Mama said it was time to go to bed.

* * *

He was in a huge open field. In the bright moonlight he could see silhouetted figures creeping closer, their guns outlined against the sky. There were hundreds of them. But he couldn't run, couldn't lift his legs. Something was holding them down. There was no feeling in them. The figures were getting closer and closer; he could see their faces. And now there were just two of them. One was Hitler! The other was Tojo, waving a sword over his head! With a groan Hugh struggled to get away. There was a yelp, and he woke up. Jiggs had gone to sleep lying on his legs.

He pushed Jiggs aside and lay there gasping, his heart pounding. He'd seen them so clearly—Hitler's mad, staring eyes. Tojo. The round black-rimmed eyeglasses, the snaggle-teeth. The sword. Hugh shuddered.

He was burning up. His pillowcase was damp with sweat. He wiped his face on the sheet and flipped his pillow to the cooler side. He closed his eyes and began to count the number of thunks the fan made. Maybe that would lull him back to sleep. He counted to forty-seven and gave up. This always seemed to happen after he had a nightmare.

He sat up. Sometimes when he had trouble sleeping it helped to go outside for a while. He slipped out of bed and put on his shorts. He picked Jiggs up so his tags wouldn't jingle and tiptoed down the stairs, surrounded by the weird blue glow of the blackout lamp.

Out on the porch he put Jiggs down. It was dark and very still. A mosquito flew into his cheek like a tiny spitball and he slapped at it. The air wasn't much cooler out here. He went down the steps and across the dunes onto the beach. He stood there for a moment, then waded out until he was knee-deep in the water. He stayed there for a while, letting the little waves eddy around his legs. Just as he turned to go back inside he saw a light, far out in the water.

Heat lightning. But no, this was different, not spread out like heat lightning. More a pinpoint of light.

Hugh caught his breath. The light out there was blinking.

A signal? Who was supposed to receive it? Was someone answering it?

He narrowed his eyes and scanned the beach from one end to the other, as far as he could see. Not a light was showing.

And then his heart skipped a beat. Suddenly another light was blinking, and it came from up the beach behind the dunes, near—his heart skipped another beat—the Spook House!

He ran out of the water and took off up the beach. Just past Mrs. Collins's house he slowed to a walk, and Jiggs peeled off to investigate something down near the water. Hugh went a little farther and climbed up onto a dune. He could just see the top of the Spook House. There in the cupola, right where he'd been the other day, he saw a light, and it was blinking, too. There was a pattern to the blinking, long and short, some sort of code. He looked out toward the horizon, but he couldn't see a thing.

Keeping low, he glided along the dunes until he was in front of the Spook House. He squatted in the sea oats and looked up at the cupola. The light was gone. He looked back out to sea. That light was gone, too. He waited a minute or so, and then he took a deep breath and began creeping toward the house.

Jiggs let out a sharp bark. Hugh threw himself back down on the sand. "Dammit, Jiggs! Now you've ruined everything!" he hissed. He scrambled up and raced back over the dunes toward home.

They were almost back to the house when Hugh saw another light. It was in his parents' room. Mama hadn't even bothered to close the blackout curtains. He broke into a run.

At the house he grabbed Jiggs and tiptoed inside. He'd tell Mama that Jiggs had wanted to go out. But when he got to the top of the steps, Tom was standing there.

"I had to let the dog out," Hugh said, "he—"

"Sally's sick," Tom said. "Your mother said not to go in."

Just then Mama came out of Sally's room. Her face was white.

"Mama—"

"Go back to bed, Hugh. You too, Tom," she said, and started downstairs. Tom went back to his room, but Hugh stayed at the top of the steps. He heard Mama giving the telephone operator a number. In a few minutes he could hear her talking, but he couldn't tell what she was saying. He figured she'd called Daddy.

Across the hall, the door to Sally's room was cracked open. Hugh pushed it far enough to see that she was lying in bed, her face turned toward the wall. He went into his parents' room and looked at the clock by the side of the bed. It was two o'clock.

The phone rang downstairs. He slipped back out into the hall. "Thank you for calling back, Dr. Coleman," Mama said. Hugh strained to hear what she was telling their pediatrician in Charleston, but he could only make out a word now and then. When Mama hung up the phone, he hurried back down the hall and climbed into bed. Jiggs was already there. He smelled terrible, but Hugh didn't care. He pulled the little dog close. Before long, they were both asleep.

Chapter Fifteen

Jiggs wasn't there when Hugh woke up the next morning. He went down the hall and peeked into Sally's room. Jiggs was stretched out on the rug next to her bed. Sally lay on her back, her eyes closed.

"Sally?" Hugh whispered.

Ever so slowly she turned her head and opened her eyes.

"Feeling better?" he said.

She didn't say anything, just closed her eyes. After a few moments, he slipped downstairs and went back to the kitchen. Mattie was crushing ice cubes wrapped in a dishtowel with a big wooden mallet. She gave the towel a couple more whacks, then put the ice into a glass and poured in some ginger ale.

"I'm going to take this up to Sally," she said. "You be quiet. Let your mama get some rest."

Hugh and Tom were the only ones at breakfast. For once Mattie didn't cook, not even toast. All they had was cold cereal and a few slices of banana. "Be glad you got that much," Mattie told them. "Can't hardly get bananas no more." She gave her head an angry shake. "This war!"

They could hear her back in the kitchen, muttering to herself. Every now and then she'd sing a line or two of a spiritual that Hugh recognized, "Nobody Knows the Trouble I've Seen." It didn't make him feel any better.

After breakfast he tried to read the paper, but he couldn't concentrate. He went out on the porch. Tom was lying in the hammock looking at a *LIFE* magazine. Hugh stood for a while staring out at the beach, not really seeing anything. He went back inside. Mama was at the dining room table, drinking a cup of coffee.

"How's—" he began.

She shook her head and took a sip of coffee. "I don't really think she's any better," she said. "She had a rough night. The aspirin I gave her doesn't seem to be working."

"You talked to the doctor?"

She rested her head on her hand. "Yes," she said. "We have to keep her quiet. Try to keep her temperature down. I'm to call him around lunchtime."

Hugh stood there for a little longer, but his mother didn't say anything more. She didn't have to. He could see how worried she was.

Sally was never sick. She had only missed one day of school last year, and that was when she had eaten way too much candy at Halloween. What could be wrong with her?

He went back outside and walked out as far as the dunes. His footprints from last night were still there. He turned back toward the house. "Tom," he called, "tell Mama I went for a walk."

The tide had left lots of shells on the beach. As he walked along, he saw sand dollars, a starfish or two, and then, next to a pile of seaweed, something Sally had been looking for all summer—a sea urchin. Very carefully he picked it up and rested it on the palm of his hand. It was perfect, all the little spikes still on it.

He thought about how Sally had looked earlier this morning, how she lay there not moving. And then all he could think of was the pictures he'd seen of children in iron lungs or wheelchairs. Once on a newsreel he'd seen President Roosevelt with polio victims over in Georgia, at Warm Springs, watching as they tried to learn to walk again with heavy braces on their legs. President Roosevelt had braces on his legs, too.

Nobody—not him or Mama or Mattie or Tom—had said the word "polio" that morning, but he knew it was what they were all thinking of. Were terrified of.

He shivered. When he tried to swallow, he almost choked. His legs were shaking. He sat down on the sand. If Sally had polio, she might be crippled. Or die.

Suddenly all of those times she'd been so obnoxious—making fun of him coastwatching or mocking H. V. Kaltenborn—didn't matter anymore. And if Sally had polio, couldn't he get it, too? His heart was beating so hard it almost hurt. He put his head between his knees and took some deep breaths. "Be okay, Sally," he whispered. "Be okay." When his breathing evened out a little, he stood and brushed the sand off his legs.

He was on his way home when he remembered the sea urchin. He'd laid it down on the sand next to him. Maybe someone else had picked it up. He raced back up the beach. It was still there.

When he got home, Mattie told him that Mama was upstairs with Sally. The bedroom door was open and Mama was leaning over her, wiping off her forehead with a wash-cloth. She straightened up and saw Hugh.

"Mama," he whispered, and she came over to the door.

He held out the sea urchin. "I found this," he said. "It's perfect. I thought it might make Sally feel better."

Mama's eyes filled with tears. Very carefully she took the sea urchin from him and put it on Sally's bedside table. And then she came back and hugged him, hard.

Chapter Sixteen

For lunch Mattie fried the shrimp that Abram had caught early that morning. Hugh ate three helpings. When he finished, he went back into the kitchen. Abram was sitting at the table.

"The shrimp was wonderful," Hugh said. "Thanks, both of you."

"You are very welcome," Mattie said.

Abram nodded. He folded his napkin carefully and laid it next to his plate. "Well, I thank you, too, Miss Mattie." He stood up. "I'll be going now."

For a moment Hugh stood at the screen door, watching Abram walk to his truck, an old black Dodge pickup with a loose back bumper and a hole in the tailpipe. You could tell from a long way off when Abram was coming.

"Abram! Wait," Hugh called, and ran down the steps.

Abram turned, one foot on the running board. "What you want, Hugh?"

"Have you heard anything more? You know—"

Abram frowned. "Oh. About them Germans?" He opened the door and crooked his finger at Hugh. "Look here." Lying along the floor of the truck, underneath the seat, was a shotgun. "Your granddaddy left me this in his will," Abram said. "I've cleaned it up good." He stroked the shining barrel with his long forefinger. "If there's any trouble, I'm ready."

Hugh felt a little thrill of fear. "Abram. I think something might be going on at the Spook...at that deserted house up beyond Mrs. Collins's place. I saw—"

"You stay away from there, son. Your mama and daddy have enough to worry about right now without you getting yourself in trouble." Abram swung himself up into the truck and closed the door. He cranked the engine, and the old truck shuddered to life.

"Abram!" Hugh jumped up onto the running board and stuck his head in the window. "I saw lights—"

Abram put the truck in reverse. "Like I say, mind you don't do anything your daddy'd frown on. Now get down, Hugh, I got to go."

* * *

"Want to go crabbing?" Tom said.

"What?" Hugh was sitting at the card table reading the newspaper. The Allies would be invading Italy any day now. He was only halfway through the article, but when he looked up at Tom, something about the expression on his cousin's face made Hugh put the paper down.

"Tide's probably too low," he said. "Hold on a minute." He went and checked the tide chart tacked to the wall next to the back door. When he came back in the living room, he told Tom, "It's too early, but heck, let's go anyway. At least it'll give us something to do."

Hugh was glad for an excuse to go outside. Sally wasn't feeling any better. She had a bad headache and her throat was sore. Mama had asked the boys to stay as quiet as possible. They couldn't even turn on the radio.

"I'll run up and tell Mama we're going," Hugh said.

She was lying on the twin bed next to Sally's, her arm over her eyes. Sally was asleep. Hugh tiptoed over to Mama and whispered, "We're going out on the dock." She nodded.

* * *

In the creek, the tide was just beginning to turn. Little fiddler crabs were scurrying around on the black mud below the dock.

"It'll be a while," Hugh said. "Want to wait?"

"Yeah."

They sat on the benches, across from each other. It was hot, but there was a little breeze, and a roof shaded this part of the dock. For a while neither of them said anything. On top of the roof a bird began making an ugly racket. Tom looked up and frowned.

"Purple grackle," Hugh said. He got up and banged on the roof with the handle of the crab net. The grackle squawked and flew off. "He'll be back," Hugh said.

They sat quietly again, not talking. The incoming tide lapped against the pilings. Then Tom said, "I hope Sally's going to be okay."

Hugh nodded. He blinked and swallowed hard.

Tom cleared his throat. His voice was a little shaky. "It'll be good to see Joe—my brother," he said. "Sometimes he gives me a hard time. But...I...I guess I miss him."

"Sometimes Sally's a pain, too," Hugh began, but it sounded all wrong now. He tried again. "But she's okay—most of the time." He still couldn't get it right. He sighed and changed the subject. "I guess you miss your father, too," he said.

Tom nodded.

"I'm sorry," Hugh said.

Tom looked at him. His eyes were the color of the sky. "Don't worry about it," he said. "Lots of other people's fathers are away. Besides, Daddy really wants to be on a ship."

"What I meant...what I'm sorry about...you know, the other night, when I was blabbing about all those ships getting torpedoed—"

Tom shrugged. "It's all right," he said. "I was kind of homesick right then." He stuck his hands in his pockets and took a deep breath. "And a friend of mine...his brother got killed. His ship..." He cleared his throat. "I was thinking about that." He picked a piece of oyster shell up off the floor and threw it out into the mud.

Hugh got up and walked over to the edge of the dock. The creek was up over the mud now, but it would still be a while before they could drop in their crab lines. He turned back toward Tom. "I think there're Germans in the Spook House," he said in a rush.

Tom frowned. "What do you mean, 'Germans'? And why

would they want to go in that dump anyway?"

"I don't know why," Hugh said. "But last night I saw a blinking light coming from that little room on top of the house. And another light out at sea."

"You mean like someone was sending a message?" asked Tom.

"Maybe. By the time I got near the house, the lights were gone. Then Jiggs barked and ruined everything."

Tom stared at Hugh as if he didn't know whether to believe him or not. Hugh braced himself for a sarcastic remark, but instead Tom said, "Why do you think it's Germans?"

And then Hugh told Tom everything—about the periscope, the cigarettes, the map, the raft, the vegetables stolen from Henry's truck.

For a little while Tom didn't say anything. He leaned out over the railing, staring down into the water as if he thought a crab might show up.

Hugh waited for him to say, "Oh, you're always seeing something," just like Sally had. But then Tom turned and looked straight at him.

"Want to go check it out?" he said.

Hugh stood there with his mouth open. "You mean go back inside the house? I don't know—" Just a few hours ago Abram had said to stay away.

"Well, maybe we wouldn't go in the house. But we could—"

"We could spy on them from the Flemings' house."

"Where's that?" Tom said.

"Next door to the Spook House, but it's not really all that

close. And the Flemings aren't there now. They went home a couple of weeks ago."

The grackle was back. Tom picked up the crab net and banged on the roof. He put the net down and looked at Hugh. "Let's go."

Chapter Seventeen

They jogged along the road and turned in at the Flemings' driveway. From the parking area a long boardwalk ran up to the house through a tunnel of scrub oaks and myrtles. They were about halfway along the boardwalk when Hugh stopped.

"There," he said, pointing to a place where a brush fire had left a patch of dead undergrowth. Through the wind-twisted tree trunks, the boys could just make out bits of the Spook House's side porch.

Suddenly Tom jumped down off the boardwalk and started picking his way through the tangled undergrowth.

"Hey!" Hugh called softly. "Take it easy! And be quiet." He followed, pausing every few steps to push aside the prickly vines that grabbed at his bare legs.

He caught up with his cousin at the edge of the thicket. Tom eased a branch aside, and they stood studying the Spook House.

"Look!" Hugh whispered. "That window!" One of the living room windows was open. The rusty screen was propped up against the porch wall.

Tom let the branch swing back. "When we were here before, none of the windows were open, were they?" he said.

Hugh shook his head. "No. Remember? We went around checking to see. The only thing open was the kitchen door."

"Right."

Between them and the side porch there was a stretch of sand littered with dead palmetto fronds and a few clumps of tall grass. An old Coke bottle stuck up out of the sand next to a huge palmetto tree.

Tom looked over at Hugh. "Ready?" he whispered.

But before Hugh could say anything, Tom had crept out of the thicket and was slithering across the sand. After a few yards, he stopped behind the palmetto tree and lay very still. Then he inched forward again. Watching him, Hugh thought about newsreels he'd seen of Marines fighting somewhere in the Pacific—on one of those islands like Guadalcanal—how they moved ever so slowly toward hidden Japanese gun emplacements.

He took a deep breath, got down on his belly, and slid out of the thicket. Every few feet he stopped and checked to be sure the coast was clear. Tom was waiting for him under the porch. They rested there for a moment. Both of them were covered with sweat and sand. Tom pointed under the house and raised his eyebrows. Hugh nodded.

They crouched underneath the house, listening. For a few moments they didn't hear anything except the whine of the mosquitoes that were circling their heads. Hugh started to slap at one, but Tom grabbed his hand. He shook his head and put his finger to his lips.

They stayed perfectly still a long time—at least it *seemed* like a long time—but they couldn't hear any sounds inside. It was hot down there under the house, and smelly, a nasty sweet smell. The mosquitoes were getting worse and worse. Finally Hugh shrugged. "Ready to go?" he whispered.

Just then they heard a rumbling noise—it sounded like a bunch of people coming down the stairs. Then they heard footsteps in the living room. Someone—a man—laughed. There were voices, more men, but Hugh couldn't make out anything they were saying. It sounded like they were gargling.

"I think maybe you're right," Tom whispered. "About them being Germans."

"You understand them? That's what they're speaking?"

"Heck, no, I don't understand, but I know it's not English. What else could it be except German?"

"I knew it!" Hugh could feel his pulse throbbing in his neck. "Now what do we do?"

"Looks like we're stuck here," said Tom. "They might see us if we try to leave."

So the boys squatted there listening and waiting, for hours, it seemed. The Germans, if that was who they were, stayed in the living room. The voices grew louder. Then there was a crash, like a piece of furniture being knocked over, and the sound of scuffling. A heavy thump. Grit and dust seeped down from the floorboards overhead. Hugh stifled a sneeze.

"Sounds like they're fighting," Tom whispered.

"Yeah, and I think it's time for us to get out of here." Hugh started easing toward the back of the house.

They were almost to the spot where the back porch stuck out from the house when Hugh's foot came down on something soft and squishy. He jerked his foot away and almost gagged when he saw what it was—the remains of a huge wharf rat. *That* was where the nasty sweet smell was coming from. He scraped his shoe back and forth in the sand, trying to get the mess off. Up ahead, Tom was waiting for him.

Here under the back porch, all was quiet. Up in the front of the house things seemed to be quiet, too. Hugh wiped his nose against his shirtsleeve to try to get rid of the dead-rat smell, but it didn't work.

"Let's go," Tom whispered. They dashed out from under the porch and flew down the driveway. They didn't stop running until they were back on the road.

They'd just gotten back to the dock and were gathering up the crabbing gear when they heard a car pulling into their driveway. Hugh turned. It was Daddy. What was *he* doing here?

Hugh dropped the crab lines and took off toward the house.

Chapter Eighteen

Before they went inside, Hugh and Tom stopped long enough to make a detour under the house to rinse off the sand—and the blood from the long scratches those vines in the thicket had ripped into their legs. Hugh left his smelly tennis shoes on the steps.

By the time they got in the house, Daddy was upstairs. They stood at the foot of the steps, waiting. Mama came down first. She frowned. "Where *were* you? I looked back at the dock, and you were gone—"

"We just went down the road a little way," Hugh said quickly, "to see the—baby herons." Suddenly a queasy feeling came over him. It was time to stop lying, time to tell his parents about the men down at the Spook House.

But Mama had already turned away. Daddy was coming down the stairs. "Hey, boys," he said, and then he looked at Mama. "What do you think?"

"Well, actually, she seems a little better than she did when I called you," she said. "Not nearly so listless. Why don't I take her temperature again, and then we'll decide." She went back up the stairs.

Hugh looked at Daddy. "Decide?"

"Whether to take her into Georgetown," he said, "to the emergency room." He heaved a huge sigh and headed toward the kitchen. "Let's get something to drink." He took off his seersucker jacket and his tie and hung them on the back of a kitchen chair. His shirt was soaked with sweat. "Hugh, how about opening us up some Cokes?" he said. He went over to the sink and splashed cold water on his face and neck.

They sat down at the table. Hugh cleared his throat. In a minute he would tell Daddy about the spies. But first he had to find out what was going on with Sally.

"What's happened?" he said. "While Sally and Mama were resting, Tom and I...we went out on the dock, and then we...and then all of a sudden, there was your car."

Daddy took a long swallow of Coke. "Your mother called about three o'clock. Sally's temperature was almost a hundred and five. I got in the car and came."

His law partner had given him some extra coupons so he could buy gas. "I drove seventy miles an hour the whole way," he said. He took another swallow and put the Coke bottle down. "I could use a *real* drink."

"You're not going to believe this." Mama was standing in the door. "Her temperature's down to below a hundred and one," she said, her voice shaking. "She says she feels better. She wants to see the boys."

Daddy stood up and put his arms around Mama. Hugh could hardly bear to look at them. When he glanced over at Tom, he was busy looking out the back window.

Hugh waited until his parents drew apart. Mama's face

was wet. Daddy pulled a handkerchief out of his back pocket and gave it to her. She was dabbing at her eyes when Hugh asked, "Can we go see her?"

His parents looked at each other. Mama nodded. "Just as far as the door," she said. "And just stay a minute."

At first Tom hung back, but Hugh said, "Come on. She said 'the boys.' That's both of us."

When they got to her door, Sally was propped up on her pillows, the sea urchin cradled in her hand.

"Hey," she said.

"Hey," Hugh said. Tom wiggled his fingers at her.

"I feel lots better," she said, but her face was bright pink and her eyes looked droopy.

"Great." The two boys said it together.

Sally held up the sea urchin. "Thanks for this."

"Glad I found it," Hugh said.

"What have y'all been doing?" she said. "Since I...you know..."

Hugh and Tom looked at each other. Hugh nodded. Then the words came tumbling out. They took turns telling her about the Germans and the Spook House and the fight. Hugh even told her about the map he had found. Sally hung onto every word.

"Do Mama and Daddy know?" she asked.

"Not yet," Hugh said. "I was getting ready to tell them, but—"

"Wait," she said. "Don't tell them yet. I want—"

"Boys," Mama called from downstairs. "That's long enough."

Sally pulled herself higher up on her pillows. Now her

eyes were wide and shining. "Please. Promise me you won't do *anything*," she whispered. "I'll be okay tomorrow. And then I can go there with you!"

"Hugh!" Mama called.

"Yes ma'am."

"Ask Sally if she needs anything."

He looked at Sally. She shook her head. And then she smiled and put her finger to her lips.

Chapter Nineteen

The bed creaked as Jiggs jumped down. Hugh woke up. It was the middle of the night, but the lights were on in the hall and Daddy was coming out of his and Mama's room. He was dressed. He came and sat down on the side of Hugh's bed.

"We've got to take Sally into Georgetown," he said. "Her temperature's way up. She and Mama are already out in the car." He rubbed his forehead. "We've talked to Mrs. Collins, and she says you and Tom can come up there."

"We'll be okay here." It was Tom, standing in the doorway.

For a minute Daddy didn't say anything. Then he took a deep breath. "Will you promise to call Mrs. Collins if—"

"Yes sir," Tom said.

"What time is it?" Hugh asked.

"Three o'clock." Daddy said.

Hugh sat up. "Does Sally have polio?"

"I hope not, Hugh," Daddy said. "I pray not." He stood up and put his hand on Tom's shoulder. "All right, Tom, you're in charge. Lock up behind us. I'll let Dot Collins know you're staying here. Call if you need her. Mattie'll be here at seven-thirty." He gave Hugh a hug. "God bless, son. We'll call as soon as…" His voice trailed off. He cleared his throat. "We'll be in touch."

Hugh got out of bed and followed Daddy as far as the stairs. He sat down on the top step and listened to his father talking to Mrs. Collins on the phone in the hall downstairs. Hugh heard the back door close. He ran to the window at the end of the hall and watched as the car pulled out onto the road. He stood there until the taillights were out of sight.

"Want to come sleep in my room?" Tom was standing behind him.

Hugh nodded. He went into Tom's room and climbed into the twin bed across from his cousin's. "You okay?" Tom asked.

"Yeah," Hugh said, but he wasn't. He lay down and closed his eyes, but his heart was banging so hard he felt like it was going to knock him out of bed. He tried taking deep breaths—in slowly, then out. In…and out. He prayed harder than he'd ever prayed before. "Please God, don't let Sally have polio. Please, God. Please." He didn't realize he'd said it out loud until he heard Tom's soft "Amen."

* * *

Hugh woke up. The phone was ringing. It was daylight, just barely. He raced downstairs and picked up the phone.

"You two all right?" Daddy asked.

"Yes sir." Hugh rubbed his eyes. "What time is it now?"

"Early. Six-fifteen. Sorry, but Mama was worried—"

"That's all right. We're fine. How's Sally?"

"A little better."

"Is it polio?"

"The doctors don't know yet, but they seem…hopeful. They're doing tests."

"When will you be home?"

"I don't know, son. But one of us will come back later this morning. And Mattie will be there soon."

"Okay."

"Love you, Hugh. Go back to sleep."

"Love you, Daddy."

Hugh sat by the phone, yawning. Jiggs nudged his leg with his nose and whined. Hugh got up and opened the screen door, and Jiggs shot across the porch and down the steps.

The sky was gray. The ocean was gray. Through the clouds, Hugh could just make out the pale disk of the sun edging up over the horizon. A hot little breeze was blowing in from the mainland, bringing with it the tiny gnats called "no-see-ums." Right away they were swarming around Hugh's head. He batted them away. Amazing how anything so teeny could make you itch so bad.

He yawned again, so hard his jaw gave a little *pop*. For a minute he stood rubbing his jaw, and then he went back inside and up to his room. He lay down on his bed and closed his eyes.

"Was that your father on the phone?"

Hugh opened his eyes. Tom was standing by his bed.

"Yeah."

"Any news?"

"They're doing tests. They're…they're…hopeful."

Tom walked over to the window and looked out. "Gloomy day."

Hugh closed his eyes again. He wished Tom would go away and let him sleep. It was so early...

"Hugh?"

He pretended to be asleep.

"Come on, Hugh. I know you're awake," Tom said. "Those men at the Spook House. How do you think they got there? On that raft you saw?"

Hugh didn't move.

"How about that map? You think that belonged to them?" Tom bent over and spoke right into Hugh's ear. "Want to go over there now and see what's going on?"

Hugh's eyes flew open. He thought about yesterday, about those voices. The fight... "I don't know—"

"Well, I think I'll go—"

Hugh raised his head. "Wait," he said.

"See you outside."

In no time Hugh was dressed and downstairs. Tom was waiting on the porch. Hugh whistled for Jiggs so he could put him inside, but the dog didn't come. Who knew where he was or when he'd be back.

The boys ran down the road to the Flemings', took the boardwalk to the thicket, and jumped off. This time Tom was prepared. He'd brought his pocketknife to cut away the vines.

In the gray light the Spook House looked scarier than ever. Everything was quiet and very still. The birds weren't even stirring yet.

"What do you think?" Tom whispered.

"Let's go 'round to the back."

They went back out onto the road and turned in at the entrance to the Spook House. Slowly they made their way up the driveway, through the tall weeds and grass. When the back of the house was in sight, they stopped and crouched behind a clump of Spanish bayonets, being care-ful—very careful—to stay away from the dagger-sharp points at the end of the long, stiff leaves.

"Sure is quiet," Tom said softly. "Maybe they've gone."

"Where to?" Hugh said. "I mean, how? Do you think somebody rescued them?" And suddenly he realized he *wanted* those Germans to be there. It didn't matter how scary they were—he wanted to see them.

"Or maybe they're around here somewhere," Tom said.

"Around here?" Hugh started and felt the prick of a Spanish bayonet against his chest. He jerked back and sat down, hard.

"What do you think you're doing?" Tom was glaring at him.

"Nothing." Hugh got up on his knees and looked all around—at the house, the thickets on either side of the property, the driveway they'd just come down. He didn't see anything suspicious. Still...

"Maybe this wasn't such a good idea—" he began.

"Oh, come on, don't chicken out. You're the one who dis-covered them."

Hugh looked back up at the house. Nothing was moving. Just the no-see-ums. He pinched one that had landed on his earlobe. Up in the tall palmetto tree next to the house, a red-winged blackbird began to whistle.

"Look," Tom said, "the upstairs windows in the back room. They're all open. That's the room with the bunk beds.

I bet the Germans are up there, asleep."

Hugh wrinkled his nose, remembering the mattresses on those bunk beds, how they were black with mildew.

Tom stood up. "Coming?" He raced up the driveway and disappeared under the porch steps. Hugh looked around one more time, and then he joined Tom under the steps. They hunkered down, listening. Not a sound, except for the blackbird's whistle and the murmur of the surf out beyond the dunes.

They eased out from under the steps, tiptoed up onto the porch, and flattened themselves against the wall. Tom pressed his hand against Hugh's chest and mouthed, "Stay here." He edged around the corner of the house. In a moment his hand appeared, beckoning to Hugh.

When he got around the corner, Hugh pointed at the floor up ahead. "Watch out for that hole," he whispered. Just beyond the hole was the rusty screen, the one they'd noticed the day before.

They looked at each other. Tom pointed forward and raised his eyebrows. Hugh nodded. They dropped to their hands and knees and began creeping along the porch. When they got to the window, Tom raised up and peeked in.

"See anything?" Hugh whispered.

Tom shook his head. "It's pretty dark in there." Then, before Hugh could stop him, he climbed in through the open window.

Hugh stood frozen. He clenched his fists, took a deep breath, and climbed in behind Tom.

They stood for a moment just inside the window, letting their eyes adjust to the dimness. Hugh's heart was beating so hard he was sure Tom could hear it. The smell of stale cigarette smoke and spilled beer and burnt food almost made him gag.

The room was a wreck—upended tables and chairs, playing cards and poker chips scattered everywhere. Cigarette butts ground into the floor. In the fireplace, squashed beer cans and a blackened saucepan, tilted on its side. There was a noise, a sort of buzzing...

And then Hugh saw him.

Chapter Twenty

Aman lay sprawled on his back on the filthy sofa. His mouth was open, and he was snoring.

Hugh and Tom edged closer to the sofa.

Even in the faint light Hugh could see that the man's lower lip was puffed out and crusted with blood. A line of drool inched down his chin.

"Is he unconscious?" Hugh whispered.

"Don't know."

"You think the others are upstairs? In the bunks?"

"Maybe." Tom went to the hall door and stood with his head cocked, listening. Hugh checked the man on the sofa. He hadn't moved. Hugh tiptoed over and stood next to Tom.

The house seemed full of noise now, ticking, bumping, thumping. The German on the sofa, snoring. And then Hugh realized the ticking was the scratch of palmetto fronds against a window, the bump a loose shutter, the thumping—his heart.

The man on the sofa groaned and turned onto his side.

His eyelids fluttered and his eyes opened. Hugh caught his breath. The man seemed to be looking straight at them. But then his eyes closed. He touched his swollen lip with the tip of his tongue and moaned. Within a few moments, he was snoring again.

Hugh let out his breath. "We'd better go," he whispered, but Tom had turned away and was walking back toward the kitchen. He moved as quietly as a cat.

"Tom!" Hugh's whisper seemed like a shout. The room was cool, but suddenly his face was slick with sweat. He wiped his forehead on his shirtsleeve, checked the man on the sofa one more time, and followed Tom.

In the dining room the Germans had been using the shells that decorated the old seine net for target practice. The ammunition must have been the ancient tennis ball that was lying on the floor among the shattered sand dollars and sea urchins. The starfish Hugh had noticed when they were there before lay on the dusty table. Someone had snapped all its legs off. Hugh shuddered.

Tom was standing in the door to the kitchen. He held up his hand. As Hugh looked over Tom's shoulder, he saw why Tom had motioned for him to stop.

A drawer was upside down on the counter, and utensils were scattered all over the floor—rusted spoons and forks, a bent can opener, an old eggbeater.

"They sure are slobs," Tom said.

"Yeah. Listen, we've got to get out of here." Hugh pointed at the back door.

They began to pick their way through the mess on the floor. Hugh was almost to the door when he came to a dead stop. He saw something just inside the pantry—something that looked familiar.

When he moved closer for a better look, his mouth fell open. It was a black rubber bag with a zipper across the top, exactly like the one he'd found at the inlet, except about twenty times bigger.

He knew they needed to get away from this place, but he couldn't take his eyes off the bag. "Tom!" he called in a loud whisper. "Look at this!"

Tom was already at the back door. "What? We gotta go!"

"I know, but wait a minute!" Hugh squatted down in front of the bag and tugged at the zipper pull. It didn't move.

Tom hesitated, then came over to the pantry.

"I can't do it," Hugh said. "I'll hold onto the bag and you try to unzip it."

Tom knelt down beside him, grabbed the zipper pull with both hands, and gave it a jerk. It moved maybe half an inch. Another jerk, another inch. Tom stopped and took a deep breath. He nodded toward the dining room "You'd better go over there and check."

Hugh tiptoed across the littered floor to the dining room door and stood there for a moment, listening. All he heard was the murmur of the ocean, the screech of a gull.

When he got back to the pantry the bag was almost open. One last jerk and Tom sat back on his heels, rubbing his right thumb.

"You okay?" Hugh said.

"Yeah." Tom gave his hand a shake. He reached inside the bag and felt around. "There's a handle," he said. "I think it's a suitcase." He tugged hard on it, but then he shook his head. "It's heavy as lead. Let's see if we can push the bag away."

"Maybe we'd better go—"

"Shut up and help me!"

Hugh grabbed one side of the bag and pushed on the thick rubber. Slowly they peeled the bag back. Their chests were heaving by the time they finally managed to free the suitcase. It was brown leather, with two straps across the top. The boys didn't have to say a word. In no time they'd unbuckled the straps and opened the suitcase.

Clothes. Folded shirts, underwear, pajamas. Rolled up socks. Hugh shook his head and scowled. "Sorry. I don't know what I thought might be in there." He got up. "Let's go."

But Tom was feeling along the sides of the suitcase, under the clothes. "There's something under here," he murmured. He pulled out a handful of wood shavings. He shook the shavings out of his hand and starting taking the clothes out of the suitcase. Suddenly Tom jerked back, like he'd been punched in the chest. "Oh my God!"

Hugh peered over Tom's shoulder.

The bottom of the case was filled with long reddish cylinders. Hugh swallowed. "Dynamite?"

Tom nodded.

Stick after dark red stick, each with a wick in one end. Just like the dynamite in cartoons. The sticks were about a foot long and as big around as a dill pickle. They were arranged in neat rows, lying in a nest of the wood shavings. There must have been fifty of them.

Tom crammed the clothes back in the suitcase and closed

it. "Let's get the heck out of here!" He got up and headed toward the back door.

"Wait," Hugh whispered. "Don't you think we ought to take one? To show—"

"I'm not touching one of those things," Tom said. He had just grabbed the doorknob when they heard a board creak over their heads. Someone was walking around upstairs.

Hugh's heart was racing so fast he felt dizzy. "Hurry, Tom!"

Tom had both hands around the rusty doorknob, twisting it as hard as he could and pulling on the door.

"Tom!"

"I'm trying as hard as I can," he gasped. "It won't move." He tried one more turn, and then he held up his hands. His palms were bleeding. "It's no use. It's stuck."

"It opened the other day!"

"Well, it's not opening today." Tom wiped his hands on his shorts. "We'll have to go out the front. Come on!" He headed toward the dining room.

For a moment Hugh stood frozen. He couldn't move. But his heart was racing, and so was his mind. What if they got caught? What would those people do to them? He shuddered again, remembering that starfish in the dining room with its legs snapped off.

Upstairs, more footsteps. Hugh took off across the kitchen, not caring that forks and spoons went skittering in every direction.

By the time he got to the living room Tom was already halfway out the window. Hugh was almost there when he slipped on a poker chip and went sprawling. The man on the sofa groaned. In just a second, Hugh was up and at the window, throwing his leg over the windowsill. Tom grabbed his arm and pulled him through. They went tearing down the porch. Someone yelled, "Halt! Halt!" Hugh looked back over his shoulder for a second. A man was leaning out of the window.

And then Hugh felt a terrific jolt. He'd fallen again. His foot, his whole leg, had gone through the hole in the floor. "Tom!" he yelled. Tom hurried back, grabbed him under the arms, and yanked him out. Hugh thought he might have screamed, but he wasn't sure.

Now more voices were shouting, but this time Hugh didn't look back. He flew down the porch after Tom. They rounded the corner, leaped off the back steps, and raced across the yard and down the driveway. They didn't stop running until they turned onto the road toward home, where they stopped for a moment and stood leaning over, their hands on their knees, gasping for breath.

And then they heard a noise—a sputtering, clanging noise. It was coming closer and closer.

Chapter Twenty-One

They ran toward Abram's truck, waving their arms and shouting. Abram slowed and pulled into Mrs. Collins's driveway. Hugh jumped up on the running board. "Abram!"

"Hugh? What are you boys—"

"Germans!" Tom shouted.

"At the Spook House!" Hugh was so winded he could hardly talk. "We saw some of them…they have dynamite!"

Abram grabbed Hugh's arm so tight it hurt. "Now you listen here. You and Tom get on up there to Miz Collins's house and tell her to call the sheriff."

"But Abram! We've got to go back. They'll get away!"

"Abram's going to take care of that. Now you and Tom do what I say. Right now!" He gave Hugh a little push so he had to jump down. Then he put the truck into reverse, backed out onto the road, and went roaring off. It was the fastest Hugh had ever seen him drive.

* * *

Mrs. Collins was in the kitchen just taking a sip of coffee when Hugh banged on her screen door. She jumped, and coffee sloshed down the front of her silky pink bathrobe.

"Hugh!" She hurried over and unlatched the door. "Come on in, both of you. What's wrong? Is it Sally?"

"No!" Hugh yelled. "It's—it's—call the sheriff! Quick!"

"Don't yell, Hugh," she said, dabbing at the front of her bathrobe with a dishtowel. "Why in the world do you need the sheriff? Where are your parents?"

"Still in Georgetown. Mrs. Collins, please, call—"

Tom took over. "You've got to hurry, Mrs. Collins. There're some Germans hiding out up at that deserted house. Abram's gone up there with a gun."

Mrs. Collins stood staring at Tom, her mouth open. Then she dropped the dishtowel and rushed out into the hall. She picked up the receiver from the telephone hanging on the wall. "Amelia," she said to the operator, "get me the sheriff."

Hugh thought about the man on the porch and the young man asleep on the sofa. Then he pictured Abram with his gun. It dawned on him that someone could get hurt...or killed.

"Yes, at the old Wilcox place, next to the Flemings'. And hurry!" She hung up and turned back to Hugh and Tom.

"Thanks, Mrs. Collins," Hugh said. "We have to go."

"Hugh! You can't! Come back here!"

But the boys were already out the back door.

* * *

Abram's truck was parked halfway up the driveway to the Spook House. The door was hanging open. The shotgun was gone. Hugh and Tom stood by the truck for a few moments, listening, and then they started moving slowly up the driveway, keeping low.

Suddenly a dog began to bark furiously. "Jiggs!" Hugh said. He broke into a run, with Tom right behind him.

They rounded the curve and there was Abram, his shotgun pointing straight at the three men who stood on the back steps, their arms raised above their heads. Jiggs was barking like a maniac. Where had he been all this time?

"Hush up, dog!" Abram shouted, and Jiggs did, except for a low growl deep in his throat.

"Abram? You okay?" Hugh called.

Abram didn't move. "Get back, Hugh!" he shouted. "Don't come no farther."

Hugh looked hard at the Germans. These men might be the enemy, but right now they didn't look very dangerous. One was wearing a suit but no shoes. Another had on pants and a vest with nothing under it. And the third had on fancy black-and-white shoes and his undershorts. He was holding a pair of pants up in front of him. And squirming. The no-see-ums were after him. Hugh almost felt sorry for him.

"Abram," Hugh called. "There's another one! Inside! He's hurt. Do you want me to—"

"You stay right there, Hugh," Abram shouted.

"Abram! Abram!" Mrs. Collins was coming down the driveway. "I called the sheriff!"

"You go back home, ma'am," Abram shouted over his shoulder. "This ain't no place for a lady like you." But Mrs. Collins marched right up in her pink bathrobe and put her arms around Hugh and Tom and held them tight.

Chapter Twenty-Two

A sheriff's deputy drove Hugh and Tom back home. The minute the boys got out of the car, Mattie started yelling at them from the top of the steps. "Where you two been! Why you want to scare old Mattie? You, Hugh! You, Tom!" But her voice was shaking, and she was wiping away tears with her apron.

The deputy started up the steps along with the boys, but he stopped halfway, apparently satisfied that they were in good hands. He tipped his hat to Mattie and hurried back to his car.

Mattie took one look at Hugh's bloody leg and rushed him into the kitchen. She pushed him down in a chair, washed off his shin, and painted it with Mercurochrome. As she bandaged it, she blessed both of them out. "How could you go off like that, meddling in something that was none of your business?" she demanded.

They kept trying to explain what had happened, but she wouldn't listen. "Abram was a hero," Tom said. "He—"

"Don't care nothing 'bout that," Mattie said. "Old Abram can take care of hisself." She jammed the stopper back on the Mercurochrome bottle and stood looming over Hugh, her hands on her hips. "Now. What y'all going to eat?"

"Eat?" Hugh said. He hadn't even thought about eating. But suddenly he was very hungry. He and Tom sat at the table and wolfed down Mattie's grits and scrambled eggs and toast.

When they finished Hugh was terribly sleepy, so sleepy he couldn't keep his eyes open.

* * *

"Hugh! Hugh! Wake up!" Mattie was standing by his bed.

He rolled over, away from her.

"Get up, Hugh!" She gave his shoulder a hard shake. "There's some men down there want to see you."

Hugh sat up, wide awake now. "Who?"

"They say they're agents. You better come on."

"Agents!"

"FBI, that's what they say. Now get moving."

When he got downstairs, two men were waiting in the kitchen, one in a dark brown suit, the other dressed in dark blue. They held their hats in their hands. Tom and Abram sat at the table. Mattie stood guard at the sink.

"This is Hugh," Mattie said when he walked in.

The men nodded at Hugh and then the one in the brown suit said, "Sit down." He didn't sound very friendly.

Back at the Spook House, Hugh and Tom had told the sheriff everything they knew, but now the FBI agents wanted to hear it all over again. The one in the blue suit took out a pad and started taking notes. They didn't seem very interested in what Hugh was telling them until he got to the part about finding the map.

"You found a map?" the one in the brown suit asked.

"Yes sir," Hugh said. "At the inlet. It was in a little—"

"Where is it?"

"Upstairs. In—"

"Go get it," the agent said. This time he definitely didn't sound friendly.

Hugh hurried up the steps to his room and got the map from its hiding place in his scrapbook.

Nobody said a word while the agent was opening the black rubber bag. He had trouble with the zipper, just like Hugh had. Once he got the map out, he stood looking at it, frowning a little, and then he showed it to the other man. He turned back to Hugh.

"Why didn't you tell somebody about this?" he said.

"I—I didn't know..." Hugh swallowed, and looked at Abram and at Tom. Then he shook his head and shrugged. His leg began to throb. He closed his eyes and leaned his head on his hand. And then he felt Mattie's big warm arm around his shoulders. She held him pressed close to her side until he finished telling the FBI agents his story.

* * *

His parents and Sally pulled up not long after the FBI agents left. When Mama heard about what had gone on at the Spook House, she burst into tears.

"I can't believe you did this when you knew how upset

we were about Sally," she sobbed. "Why did you go into that house? What in the world were you thinking?"

Hugh's face was burning. What *had* he been thinking? The truth was that everything had happened so fast he'd hardly had time to think.

Chapter Twenty-Three

I t was Sunday afternoon. They were all out on the front porch—Mama, Daddy, Aunt Ellen, who'd arrived that morning, and Mrs. Collins. She was wearing a red dress and big hoop earrings, and her blond hair was pulled up high in a pompadour like a movie star's.

Sally lay propped up on a pillow in the hammock. She was much better. It hadn't been polio after all, but a bad viral infection. Still, the doctors said she had to take it easy for a while.

Hugh and Tom sat on the steps with Jiggs stretched out at their feet. A bandage covered Hugh's shin where the skin had ripped off when Tom pulled him out of the hole at the Spook House. It had hurt pretty bad at first, but probably not any worse than Tom's scraped hands, still faintly orange with Mercurochrome.

Sunday newspapers were strewn about on the floor. The Charleston, Columbia, and Charlotte papers all carried big headlines about the Germans caught at the Spook House. Hugh liked the headline from the Columbia paper best: FISHERMAN AND BOYS FOIL GERMAN PLOT. He'd probably read that article ten times. "Authorities are still piecing together evidence from what appears to have been an audacious plot to sabotage the Charleston Naval Base. It is known that a submarine was involved, as well as a high-ranking Nazi prisoner of war held in a camp near Myrtle Beach...."

The map Hugh had found at the inlet turned out to be a layout of the dry docks at the naval base. He'd hoped maybe the agents would give the map back to him once they'd looked at it, but of course they hadn't. One thing Hugh did not mention—the cigarette package the crab had brought up. It stayed hidden deep in the pages of his scrapbook.

"Well, we'll be going now." Mattie was standing at the door to the porch, Abram looking over her shoulder.

"Oh, Mattie!" Mama got up and hurried to the door. "You all have to get back to church, don't you?"

Mattie nodded. "In a little while."

"I can't thank you enough for all you did—"

"Didn't do much. But them *little* boys over there about scared this old woman to death. Going off like that. You hear me, Hugh? You, Tom?"

"I'm sorry, Mattie," Hugh called. He'd already told her that about a thousand times.

"Me too," Tom said. He didn't bother to look around.

"Come on, Miss Mattie," Abram said. "Good evening, all." He led his wife away. In a few minutes, his old truck was sputtering to life behind the house.

"Mattie's right. We should have kept a better eye on you two," Daddy said. "As clumsy as those fellows were, they were also extremely dangerous."

"Everything turned out okay," Hugh murmured. Still...he hadn't told a soul that after the FBI agents left, he'd gone up to his room and huddled just inside the door, shaking so hard his teeth chattered.

"No more monkey business, okay?" Daddy said.

"Yes sir. No more monkey business." Hugh felt a nudge in his ribs. Tom was looking at him, smiling a little.

"Pretty amazing," Daddy said. "A seventy-five year old, two boys, and a cocker spaniel—the Island Army." He looked over at Mrs. Collins. "And a cheering section." She smiled and gave her head a waggle that set the huge hoops in her ears to swaying.

* * *

Everyone had gone inside except for Hugh. He stood leaning on the porch railing, thinking about everything that had happened. It had all started with the periscope and the prisoners of war out on the beach, especially the one who'd stood in the surf looking up at the Spook House. Was he the "high-ranking Nazi"? He remembered the raft in the reeds, the blinking lights he'd seen in the middle of the night, the Germans standing on the steps with their hands up, Abram pointing his shotgun.

He thought about when he and Tom were standing in the driveway, watching the military policemen handcuff the Germans. "What do you think will happen to them?" Hugh had asked.

"They'll probably all be dead in a month," Tom had said.

A sick feeling had come over Hugh. "Why do you say that?" he'd asked.

"Because spies get executed."

Hugh hadn't asked any more questions. After they'd talked to the FBI agents, he and his cousin seemed to have come to a silent agreement to let the subject drop for a while.

Tom was leaving tomorrow, and Hugh would miss him. He hoped that nothing would happen to Tom's father. He'd started saying a little prayer for him every night. In just two weeks Hugh and Sally and Mama would be going back to Charleston. School was supposed to start the Tuesday after Labor Day if the polio epidemic had ended. They'd be telling Abram and Mattie good-bye until Thanksgiving, when they'd return to the beach for a long weekend.

The binoculars were lying on the railing next to him. He picked them up and looked out to sea.

"Still coastwatching?" It was Sally. He hadn't heard the door open. She came and stood next to him.

"No, just looking for the osprey," he said. "It's about time for his supper."

"It's time for yours, too," she said. "I came to get you."

He lowered the binoculars and looked at her. She was a little pale, and thinner, but she looked pretty good, considering how sick she'd been.

"You know what," he said, "I'm really glad you're okay. I was scared."

She sighed. "I just wish I could've been there—at the Spook House."

He shook his head. "You'd have waked up that German on the sofa in about two seconds."

She gave his arm a little tap. "Yep, I probably would

have." She turned away. "You'd better come on, now." The screen door creaked open.

"Be there in a minute." The door swung shut.

Jiggs trotted up the steps, back from his late afternoon prowl. He stopped at the top of the steps and gave himself a shake. Then he sat down and looked up at Hugh.

"Hey, boy," Hugh said. "How's it feel to be a hero?" Jiggs wagged his stubby tail.

Hugh raised the binoculars and there was the osprey, cruising low over the dark blue water, riding a current of air. Then, as fast as lightning, it plunged down like a fighter plane and *splash!* soared off with its squirming catch.

Hugh smiled. He put the binoculars down, whistled for Jiggs, and they went inside.

Author's Note

THE COASTWATCHER is fiction. Hugh's story did not really happen. But many of the details are real. The background of the story reflects how a war thousands of miles away affected daily life in a small community in the United States.

Were there really coastwatchers during World War II?

Yes. In the earliest days of the war, the Coast Guard patrolled the beaches along the eastern coast of the United States. They were assisted by volunteer groups like yacht owners and horsemen, who formed coastal patrol organizations. The Civil Air Patrol, created in December 1941, hunted for German submarines and located downed pilots and survivors of torpedoed ships. The CAP also supervised a cadet program providing military and aviation training to teenagers; this program is still in operation. In Great Britain, members of the all-volunteer Home Guard assisted the Royal Air Force as "spotters" of enemy aircraft along the coasts.

In the book, Hugh bases his "coastwatching" on a group based in the South Pacific. This network of civil servants, traders, coconut planters, missionaries, and friendly natives was particularly effective during the six-month Battle of Guadalcanal in the Solomon Islands, northeast of Australia. Often operating from deep within jungles or high on mountainsides, these coastwatchers transmitted intelligence by radio or Morse code to U.S. armed forces and their allies about movements of Japanese ships and airplanes.

Were there attacks on the eastern coast of North America during World War II?

Yes. In January of 1942, packs of German submarines—U-boats—lurking along the East Coast from Newfoundland to the Caribbean and into the Gulf of Mexico began to torpedo cargo ships loaded with oil and other essential war materials. Slow, unprotected, and brightly lit, the cargo ships were sitting ducks for the U-boats, which surfaced at night. In the first six months of 1942, several hundred U.S. freighters and tankers were lost, along with thousands of lives. Some of these attacks were so close to land

that crowds of spectators gathered on the beach to watch as the burning ships went down. After the United States instituted naval convoys, aerial surveillance,

WWII German U-boat

and blackouts of the ships and coastal areas, the attacks gradually came to an end.

Were actual "saboteurs" discovered within the United States during the war?

In June 1942, German submarines discharged eight men in rubber boats, four off Long Island, New York, and four near Jacksonville, Florida. With them were boxes full of explosives for use in sabotaging major industrial complexes. All these men had been trained by the *Abwehr*, the German intelligence agency. They had lived in the United States at one time and spoke English fluently. In spite of their training and background, however, they were all captured within two weeks and handed over to the FBI, the U.S. agency charged with investigating espionage. After trial by a military tribunal, six of the men were executed, the other two imprisoned. The "saboteurs" in THE COASTWATCHER are fictional; there is no evidence that any German agents landed in South Carolina with plans to sabotage the Charleston Naval Base.

Were there POW camps in the United States during the war?

German and Italian prisoners of war—POWs—began arriving in the United States in the spring of 1943, after the defeat of German forces in North Africa. By the end of World War II, there were more than 425,000 POWs on American soil.

German prisoners in WWII POW camp

Many prisoners were sent to the South, where they lived in camps and worked on nearby farms, helping to harvest crops and cut timber. The usual camp was either square or rectangular, surrounded by barbed-wire fences with a guard tower at each corner. At night the camps were brilliantly lit by floodlights. Most of the prisoners were hard workers and seemed content to be away from the war raging in Europe. But there were some troublemakers, often hard-core Nazis, whose *Lagergestapo,* or secret police, terrorized POWs they suspected of being less than loyal to Hitler. Government records show that this group murdered at least seven fellow prisoners over the years.

What did the people at home do to help during the war?

Almost everyone, young and old, pitched in to help with the "war effort," collecting "scrap"—everything from radiators to toothpaste tubes, from rubber tires to rubber bands—to be recycled for munitions or military vehicles. Old newspapers were used for packing material, nylon stockings for powder bags for naval guns. All over America homemakers saved the fat drippings from bacon, which could be used in making explosives. To ward off a serious

food shortage in the
United States, the government urged people to grow
their own food. "Victory
Gardens" sprang up in
backyards almost every-
where. In 1943, these gardens provided at least a
third of all the fresh vegetables consumed in the
United States.

With so many Amer-
icans serving in the war,
people at home had to fill
in the gaps in the work

DEFENSE ON THE SEA
BEGINS ON THE SHORE

WWII Defense at Sea poster

force. During the early 1940s more than six million women
went to work in war production, including jobs in arma-
ment factories, shipyards, and airplane plants.

Civil Defense volunteers served in many capacities—
some were air raid wardens, enforcing blackouts; others
called "spotters" camped on rooftops watching for enemy
airplanes. Thousands of civilians assisted the Red Cross by
rolling bandages, manning the blood banks, and visiting
wounded soldiers in hospitals.

What was rationing?

During the war, most Americans had to do without some
things. In January of 1942, the government began a compli-
cated system called rationing. Books of coupons were
issued monthly, with point values assigned to items such as

meat, butter, cheese, sugar, coffee, and shoes. Once a family had redeemed all their points for these items, they had to wait until the next month to buy more. While gas was rationed, the average driver was allowed to buy only three gallons a week.

Was polio a serious threat in the United States at the time of the war?

During the 1940s, another battle was raging—the war against polio, a viral illness that usually occurred in the summertime and killed or paralyzed thousands of children and young adults. As a young man, Franklin Roosevelt had contracted polio, which left his legs paralyzed. In the summer, when the disease was most prevalent, parents fortunate enough to be able to leave the cities took their children to places like the beach or the mountains. The polio epidemic declined after vaccines were introduced by Dr. Jonas Salk and Dr. Albert Sabin in the mid-1950s.

Is some of THE COASTWATCHER based on your own memories?

Yes. When I was a young child, World War II seemed very immediate.

My first memory of WWII was the day in December when the Japanese bombed Pearl Harbor. My twin brother and I were four years old.

The author with her brother and a little friend

The Coastwatcher

We were in the living room with our parents when the news came over the radio. What I remember most was my father's excitement. Like Hugh's father, he tried to enlist in all the armed services, but was turned down because of his poor eyesight. He ended up in India working with the American Red Cross. As an Assistant Field Director, he

The author, her brother, and their cocker spaniels

served as a contact between soldiers' families and the military. Among his duties was reporting back to families who had requested information about the health and welfare of their loved ones.

Almost everyone we knew had a relative who signed up in one of the armed forces. One of my uncles served in England, another in China.

When my brother and I went to the movie theater on Saturday afternoons, we saw scenes from the battlefront in the newsreels. When we picked up the Sunday newspaper or the latest issue of *Life* magazine, we saw pictures of soldiers fighting in the war. Almost every evening my family gathered around the radio and listened to newscasts delivered by Edward R. Murrow of CBS or by NBC's H. V. Kaltenborn, the "pioneer" of radio journalism.

A POW camp was built near the beach where my family spent summer vacations. Like Sally, I asked my parents what POW meant, rhyming it with "wow," as we rode past a group of prisoners and their guards.

Is the place where Hugh and Sally spent the summer real?

The setting of THE COASTWATCHER is imaginary. But if you've ever been to Pawleys Island, South Carolina, much of it will seem familiar.

What other sources did you use to find out about the World War II era?

As I researched the WWII era, I found the following periodicals particularly helpful: *Time Magazine, Life Magazine, The New York Times, The Atlanta Journal-Constitution, The Augusta Chronicle,* and other regional newspapers. *This Fabulous Century, Vol. V, 1940–1950,* by the Editors of TIME-LIFE Books, provided wide-ranging commentary about this period as well as invaluable photographs, including mug shots of the "Amagansett Six"—the German saboteurs on whom the spies in THE COASTWATCHER are based. I also gathered useful background information from these books: *Operation Drumbeat: the Dramatic True Story of Germany's First U-boat Attacks Along the American Coast in World War II,* by Michael Gannon; *Lonely Vigil: Coastwatchers of the Solomons,* by Walter Lord; and *Alone on Guadalcanal: a Coastwatcher's Story,* by Martin Clemens.

About the Author

ELISE WESTON is a graduate of the University of South Carolina. She has published articles and book reviews in numerous publications and is the former book page editor of *Augusta Magazine.*

THE COASTWATCHER is her first novel. She lives in Augusta, Georgia.